Curtains for the Condo Casanova

THE UNSCRIPTED DETECTIVE
BOOK 1

BARBARA BARRETT

Paperback ISBN 978-1-948532-68-6

This book is dedicated to my Florida condo neighbors: Barb and Jeff, Janice and Kayla, Erica and Ray, Diane and Chris, Arlene and Curt and Lesley and Andy. You've been there for me throughout the last fifteen years.

one

. . .

arla Dane patted the damp remains of her three-hundred-dollar haircut and sighed with resignation. She had no idea when she'd be able to afford such a luxury again. *Welcome back to Minnesota, Marla. Not exactly the homecoming you were expecting.*

Five minutes earlier, a sudden autumn downpour burst the minute she emerged from her rideshare. An hour and a half before that, she'd arrived at the Minneapolis-St. Paul Airport and then waited in vain for sixty minutes to be picked up by her sister, Kitty Lovejoy.

Where was Kitty, anyhow? It wasn't like her to be late for anything, let alone be a total no-show. Was her absence one more hint things were not as they should be with her younger sister? To make matters worse, without Kitty to let her in, she was locked out of the secure building and stranded in the rain.

Kitty had been the one to suggest an extended visit to her home state after Marla had been let go from the television show on which she'd starred for six seasons, *Carruthers on the Case,* where she'd played Letitia Carruthers, PI.

The network had convinced her showrunner that the only

way he could keep the show afloat another season was to bring in a younger cast. The title was changed to *Carruthers on the Case, The Early Years.* Some smart-aleck reporter had come up with the headline, "Letitia Carruthers Youthanized," and everyone ran with it. The media attention following her unprecedented "firing" had been brutal.

Clinging to an unreal hope that casting directors would be breaking down her door when the news got around that she was available, Marla had thanked her sister for the invite but remained in LA waiting for the offers to roll in. Even when those offers didn't magically materialize, she stayed on the West Coast, thinking the stigma of being fired would cool down eventually. But days turned into weeks, which turned into months. The new network TV season had come and gone, and she was still no part of it.

Increasingly desperate for a role, she foolishly invested a significant part of her nest egg in a project that died on the vine. Humiliated and depressed, she'd backed away from LA's social life to the point of almost becoming a recluse.

Kitty's calls became less frequent, and her urging to come join her was forgotten until Kitty's next-door neighbor, Tom Casey, called and asked Marla to reconsider Kitty's invitation. He wouldn't say why he was calling instead of Kitty, nor would he divulge why he thought a visit at this time was necessary. But his tone was definitely serious and concerned. The mystery had scared Marla enough to find a house sitter for her place in Santa Monica and head east.

A sudden gust of wind blew over a small planter next to her on the bench where she sat under the building's portico. Righting the hydrangea bush in the planter not only soaked the front of her hoodie, the action left behind several stray leaves and petals and ruined her Prada designer jeans and Tory Burch ballet flats. Before her recent troubles, she would've thrown out the damaged goods with little thought to the money going down the drain. Now, she'd have to do her best to revive them.

Just as she was about to slip even further into this morass of self-pity, a ray of sunshine showed up in the form of a woman opening the front door. She appeared to be somewhere in her mid-sixties like Marla with her gray hair cut short, bangs off to the side. "Locked out?" she asked.

Marla resisted the urge to ask why else she'd be sitting out in this downpour, her own graying red locks emerging from the hoodie, dripping water. "I'm visiting my sister, who seems to have forgotten about my arrival. And can't be reached by phone."

"We're not supposed to admit strangers to the building, but I can't let you stay out here in this deluge. Follow me. I can at least get you inside and out of this rain."

"Thanks," Marla mumbled as she attempted to carry both her bags at once.

"I'm not allowed to carry more than ten pounds or I'd get that second one. But I'll wait in the lobby to let you back in if you want to return for it."

Not much choice. Marla accepted the offer.

"Who're you visiting?" the woman asked once Marla and both bags were inside the building.

"My sister, Kitty Lovejoy."

Realization dawned in the woman's eyes. "Then you're ...?"

"Marla. Marla Dane. I used the storm to arrive incognito so I wouldn't be recognized," she joked.

Her rescuer offered her hand. "I'm Scottie Richards. Glad you still have your sense of humor. I should have recognized you even after the rain had its way with you. I loved your show. I'm sorry about ..." She didn't finish. They both knew what she meant.

Marla offered the standard reply she'd developed since she

found herself unemployed. "Thanks. I appreciate your support. But that's the name of the game in the entertainment industry. Youth sells."

"Well, this *audience* is still wanting to see more of you. There aren't that many TV shows that feature older actresses as bright, independent beings."

True. Unfortunately, the powers that be in the entertainment industry appeared completely unaware of that notion. "The right part will come along soon. In the meantime, Kitty convinced me it's time for another visit."

"And then she goes and forgets today's your arrival day." Richards angled her head, considering. "Unusual for her. She's usually on top of these details. If I could let you into her condo, I would, but I don't know her code. They warn us about over-sharing information like that."

Although tempted to follow up on Scottie's comment about Kitty's forgetfulness being so unusual, it was more important to get to Kitty's condo. "I'm just thankful you trusted me enough to let me into the building so my luggage and I can dry off before she appears."

"I know!" Scottie held up an index finger. "Tom Casey, her next-door neighbor is a friend of mine. I'll call him. He should have the code."

Tom Casey. The guy who called her with his concerns about Kitty. She should've thought of him first.

Scottie returned within a minute. "Tom wasn't home, so I contacted someone else in the building. He's a retired police officer who most of us trust with information like that. His name is Rex Alcorn. He'll be down shortly." She waited with Marla.

Almost immediately, a male form emerged from the elevator. In his charcoal-gray sweatpants and blue sweatshirt, the guy gave new meaning to the term silver fox. Over six fee t tall, he showed no sign of the prominent gut so prevalent amongst men her age. His wide-set blue-gray eyes narrowed just short of a scowl. "Gotta make this fast. Top of the fifth and the Twins are behind by one run." Only after he made this pronouncement to the world in general did he turn to Marla. "You're Kitty's older sister. I missed meeting you the last time you were in town."

"Thank you for taking pity on me in this situation. I have no idea where Kitty is," she said, attempting to get off on the appropriate friendly foot while she fought the temptation to take in this gorgeous sight.

"That why you deigned to visit her again?" he asked. "So we can all take pity on the poor millionaire actress who got the ax?"

"Uh ..."

"Be nice, Rex," Scottie said. "Kitty's disappeared and can't be reached by phone. And this poor woman got caught outside in that rain."

Rex gave her the once-over, which consisted of a brief flash of something until his eyes hooded over.

She knew that look. That male-spots-female look and likes-what-he-sees look. But it was gone in a flash.

"I see. Guess you don't have your makeup and wardrobe people at your beck and call these days."

A real sweetheart, this Alcorn.

"Today anyhow," she replied. "Could you help me with my bags?"

He disappeared without a word, returning seconds later pulling a luggage cart. "Got a bad back. Although this place isn't devoted to senior living, there are a lot of us here with that problem. That's why we keep these contraptions around."

He lifted one, then the other suitcase onto the cart, bad back and all.

"Thanks," she said, not sure what else to say.

Marla thanked Scottie, who scuttled off as soon as Rex appeared to have taken over.

Marla let him push the cart onto the elevator. Neither spoke on the way to the third floor, though she was hard-pressed not to sneak a few surreptitious glances at the man who seemed so anxious to be rid of her.

Once they arrived at the third floor, he pushed the cart off the elevator and down the spacious hallway.

He paused when they reached Kitty's condo. "What's your sister's maiden name?" he asked.

"Thatcher, the same as mine. If you weren't sure it was me, why did you wait until now to ask me that question rather than when we were in the lobby?"

"I figured you are who you say you are, but it never hurts to check. You look vaguely like the woman on the TV show although a little worse for wear today."

"I hadn't planned on getting caught in a monsoon," she replied. "Then you have watched my show. I got the impression you preferred sports to TV crime dramas."

"I do, but Kitty harassed me enough about watching it that I finally gave in just so I could get her off my back."

"What did you think of it?" she asked before she realized how needy that sounded.

"You don't want to know."

"Too grisly?"

"Grisly, no. I've seen more than my share of grisly in my life. But a sixty-something woman in designer pantsuits and stilettos chasing bad guys? Totally unbelievable."

"There was that, but what about the acting?" It was out before she thought better of asking.

"You really want to know?" he asked.

"I guess when you put it like that, no," she replied, although she couldn't help wondering what he might've said.

After what seemed like minutes but had only been seconds, he punched a code into the door lock. He opened the door for her, and she entered cautiously. What if Kitty was sick and couldn't come to her phone? Worse yet, what if ... Marla couldn't even finish that thought. She tried to rid her brain of such an image, but she'd worked with dead bodies so long, even though they were pretend dead bodies, it wasn't easy.

"Kitty?" she called as she walked tentatively through the living room, then the kitchen and dining room and finally the bedrooms. No sign of her. What she did find was Kitty's cell phone resting on the charger. This wasn't good. Maybe Tom Casey had been right to summon Marla.

"She wouldn't go anywhere without her phone," she told Alcorn.

"Apparently she did," he replied laconically. "Want me go down to the garage and see if her car is there?"

He was offering to help? Didn't he have a ball game to get back to? "Yes, okay, if you wouldn't mind."

"I assume she'll put you in her only guest room. I'll push this cart in there and unload your bags before I go down. Want 'em on the bed or elsewhere?"

Maybe he wasn't quite the jerk she thought he was at first. The verdict was still out on that one, but his status was beginning to rise in her book.

After he left, she strolled from room to room seeking some sort of clue where Kitty was. Her sister must've done some redecorating. Bright yellow met her everywhere, along with touches of red, black and purple. Soft blue had been the dominant color the last time she visited.

She found her sister's purse in her bedroom but no wallet. The phone had charged to a hundred percent. But that wasn't conclusive. Kitty could've been gone a couple of hours or just dashed out with the percent already on a high charge.

Next, she studied the contents of the fridge. Kitty had

stocked it with Marla's favorite type of soda, Diet Coke. "Pop," now that she was back in the Midwest.

Finally, she snooped in the various waste containers around the condo looking for bloodied bandages and fortunately discovered nothing of that nature. She couldn't believe she'd succumbed to something Letitia would do. Unlike Letitia, though, she hadn't been able to figure out anything about her sister's disappearance. Some detective she'd turned out to be.

Once again, she had to remind herself to stop thinking like that.

"Her car's still in its usual spot in the garage," Rex called out as he returned. "Hey, where are you?"

She emerged from the corridor leading to Kitty's bedroom. "I've been reconnoitering. Thought maybe I'd find something to suggest where she went or what happened to her, but I found nothing."

"Let a pro do that," he told her, swaggering past as he went by, presumably to check Kitty's bedroom.

He seemed to know his way around the condo. Was he a frequent visitor? Especially to Kitty's bedroom. One more question for her sister whenever she showed up.

That was exactly when the door flew open and Kitty rushed in, soaking wet. "Oh, Marla, I'm so sorry I missed you at the airport and then wasn't here to let you in." That last part made her pause. "Wait. You are in. How did you manage that?"

"That would've been me, Kitty," Rex said, coming from the bedroom hallway. "Scottie Richards found her under the portico attempting to stay out of the rain and let her in. She called me because I know the code to this place."

Kitty glanced from Rex to Marla, taking in the explanation. "I'm so glad someone let you in after that sudden shower. Look at me. I caught got in it myself." Where Marla's appearance resembled that of a soaking dog, her hair matted down with droplets of moisture still inching down her neck, Kitty, two inches shorter than Marla's five-eight, barely looked the worse for wear. Her shoulder-length blond bob just slightly glistened.

"Where were you?" Marla asked, trying not to sound accusatory.

Kitty groaned. "I got a last-minute invitation to check out Roger Halliwell's new boat over on the St. Croix River." She avoided Rex's gaze at this point, something Marla made a mental note to ask about later after Rex left. "Some new boat! New to him, so new he flooded it and then couldn't restart the motor. We sat out there drifting in the middle of the river for what seemed like ages before someone rescued us and pulled us in to shore. But not until after the rain. Everyone else was smart enough to get off the water by then."

"Why didn't you take your phone?" Rex asked a little too pointedly.

"I started to and then noticed it was down to five percent battery. And Roger forgot and left his in his car."

"Mystery solved," Rex said, "except for why you'd ever go out with Roger Halliwell in the first place."

"He had a boat, Rex. I love to be out on the water, although not after today and certainly not ever again with Roger."

Yes, there was definitely a story there. Something to discuss while they treated themselves to ice cream sundaes later. Her sister's love life seemed much more interesting at the moment than Marla's lack of new acting roles.

two

. . .

"Now that Rex has left and we have our bowls of ice cream, tell me why you're really here," Kitty said as the two of them clustered around the small island in her kitchen.

Marla pulled out the necklace she usually wore beneath her knit pullover and fingered it. It was a diamond pendant her late husband, Carson Grant, had given her at the conclusion of her first successful season of *On the Case*. She wore it all the time except when shooting the show. Touching it had become her go-to whenever she was unsure of her next steps.

She suspected she'd receive some sort of grilling from her sister because she hadn't communicated much with Kitty or anyone else since her attempt to revive her career had bombed. But she didn't want to rat out Tom Casey and his plea for Marla to come help her sister.

If only there was a reluctant or rejected lover she could tell her sister about. Kitty could relate to either situation, but failed million-dollar movie deals weren't in her sister's wheelhouse. Still, Kitty wasn't a flake. She could understand the tenets of business as well as any other Minnesotan. "I came back home to escape my life in California, Kitty."

"I assumed things were improving when you stopped complaining about all the media attention," Kitty replied. "That's why I backed off begging you to visit."

"I wasn't ready to come then. I kept believing I'd receive an offer of a part at any time. I just had to be patient."

Kitty set her spoon down. "Patience has never been one of your strong suits. Mine, neither, for that matter. We've always been women of action, wanting to fix whatever wasn't working or running with whatever challenge was in the offing." She took one of Marla's hands in hers. "Did something happen when your patience ran out?"

"That's a diplomatic way of putting it. I'd rather not get into the nasty specifics just yet. For now, let's just say I made a poor decision thinking it would improve, no, solidify my chances of securing a great part, and it didn't work out."

Kitty narrowed her eyes and gazed back at her sister. "Whatever it was doesn't sound good."

"I needed to get away from my foolishness, which is why I'm back here. I have no idea how long I'll stay, so let me know whenever you want me to move on."

"Nonsense! I've got more than enough room in this condo. It will be fun to have a roommate again."

Enough about her dilemma. Time to focus on Kitty. "How about you?" Did Kitty realize how much her neighbor, Tom Casey, was concerned about her?

Kitty took another spoonful of ice cream before answering. "What about me? Nothing's changed in my life. At least not recently."

"No problems with Gardner?"

"I don't have any problems with my ex-husband because I don't communicate with him, although every so often the kids update me about his latest girlfriend. There've been three since the one who caused our divorce."

"Is that why you've become a serial dater yourself, to keep up with him?" The question might cut, but it was important as they were getting reacquainted that Marla understand what was driving her sister's social life.

Kitty licked her spoon and set it down. "Don't worry about me. I'm enjoying a full social life. It's nice to be escorted when I go out. But I'm selective who I share my bed with."

"Sorry. I'm just trying to gauge how well you've adjusted to being single again. Big sister thing for which I won't apologize."

Kitty chuckled. "Got it. I've missed your well-meaning interest in my life. But let's get back to you, despite your attempts to make this reunion about me." She sat forward and clasped her hands together. "I know the perfect way to get you past your troubles while you're here." She offered an overly optimistic grin and waited for a response.

"That's not exactly what I had in mind by coming here, but I'll bite. What's your panacea, Dr. Lovejoy?"

"Hiding out in that big, lonely house in Santa Monica all this time has probably dulled your sense of adventure. We need to get you out into the world again, at least the world of Maple Knolls, so you can try new things."

Exactly the opposite of why she'd escaped to the Midwest. Marla didn't want new adventures. She wanted to recalibrate her life in private until the perfect part and the perfect opportunity arose. She hadn't quite given up hope of that ever happening. Her manager, Jayne Yarmouth, the closest person she'd had to a confidante these past months, suggested it wasn't unusual for actors leaving one TV show to wait at least a year before tackling another TV role.

"I can't ask you to put what appears to be your busy social

life on hold to revive mine, Kitty. Go on about your daily activities. I'll be fine on my own."

Kitty returned a skeptical look. "Do you really believe that?"

"What would you have me do, be a third wheel on your next date with Roger Halliwell?"

Kitty blew out a huff. "Like I told you, Roger is no more. In my life, anyhow." She paused long enough for her downturned mouth to curve slightly upward. "Besides, I'm moving on. There's already a new target on my horizon. But let's get back to you. I want you to come with me to my book club meeting tomorrow. Don't worry about not having read the book. Some of us rarely get that far. But we have great discussions over lunch, including the latest gossip."

Just what she wanted, gossip. The very thing that had prevented her from moving on after being released from the show. "Thanks, but I've already downloaded several bestsellers onto my notepad. I'll have my own personal book club."

"All the more reason to come to mine. You can decide whether you want to read whatever the book is we're discussing this month."

"You don't know?" Although Kitty's total lack of interest in book reading didn't surprise her, the fact that her sister was willing to let others in on her little secret was a bit of a shock.

"Don't worry. I'll google it tonight and read some of the online reviews. They'll never know I was too busy with other things the past month to read the book."

Marla eyed her sister. "I don't know whether to congratulate you on your ingenuity or lecture you about your lazy habits."

Kitty waved off her comment. "You're going with me. No more arguing. You'll love the restaurant. The chef is the son of one of the guys here in the complex."

"If I agree to go, that's it. Afterwards, I'm settling into that comfortable chair on your balcony the rest of the week with my own reading."

Kitty opened her mouth but shut it before speaking.

That was it? No more prodding? Marla would count this as a win and not pursue it further.

The next day, she realized she'd given in too soon.

Unfortunately, that insight didn't hit until after she and Kitty joined the book club group at the restaurant.

Before they even were seated, the first person to greet them was Scottie Richards. A friendly face, since she'd come to Marla's aid the day before. "Looks like you found Kitty," she said.

"Yes, not too long after you helped me get into the building, an act of kindness that was much appreciated."

Kitty took in the friendly exchange between the two women. "I wasn't there when she arrived due to circumstances beyond my control." Her defensiveness crackled.

"Oh?" Scottie replied.

Kitty skipped over her late arrival and switched gears. "I wanted my big sister to meet some of my friends while she's here. What better occasion than this group?"

A fair-skinned woman with an ash-blond ponytail joined them, her eyes wide with surprise. "Letitia? Letitia Carruthers is having lunch with us? Kitty is always telling us you're her sister, but I never thought we'd meet you in person."

"Don't call her Letitia," Kitty said, stepping between Marla and the woman. "Patty, I'd like you to meet my sister, Marla Dane. Marla, this fangirl is Patty Goodhue. She substitutes on our pickleball team."

Patty held out a hand. "Marla, then. Sorry to gush so, but

your show has given hope to women like me that there is life after fifty. And beyond, in my case."

Marla attempted to keep the smile on her face, but if the woman only knew how little "hope" she had for herself these days now that Letitia had been made younger, she'd look elsewhere for inspiration. There was no need to deflate the woman's enthusiasm, so Marla attempted to navigate her way through this new social situation, talking with someone who was both a fan and a friend of Kitty. "Thank you. I never tire of hearing from fans, even though I'm no longer with the show."

Patty wrinkled her brow. "I heard about that. What happened? Why did you walk away from such a success?"

There it was. The question that inevitably came up whenever she met someone who knew about her departure from the show. Though she'd fine-tuned a standard response during these past months, these were Kitty's friends. She hated feeding them the same line. But she'd learned the hard way that too much information could work against her.

"I wanted to bow out while we were still a hit," she said. They were still a hit; that much was true. But there was no way she wanted to bow out.

A curtain dropped down over Patty's eyes. "Oh, uh, sure."

"What do you plan to do next?" asked another woman who'd come up to them, this one svelte with short black hair in tight curls. The burnt orange bracelets on her light brown wrists matched her tunic.

And there was the second worst question Marla had been trying to avoid.

She called up the best smile in her acting repertoire. "Thanks for asking. At the moment, I'm reviewing a number of offers."

"That's why she's here visiting me," Kitty added. "So she can escape the demands of everyone out in Hollywood who's been courting her to take on their project."

Bless her sister. Though Kitty had no idea what all had been going on in Marla's life, she'd done her best to come to her defense with these women. Of course, she'd been the one who insisted Marla join their meeting in the first place, so in a way, she owed her.

"I'm Sharee Cunningham, Marla," the woman said, emphasizing Marla's name to show she was up to speed with the name thing. "I live on the same floor as Kitty. I hope we'll be seeing more of each other."

Marla merely smiled at that comment.

Scottie, Patty, Sharee. Kitty said there'd be six other women in their group. Three down, three to go.

"Just one question, Letitia, uh, Marla," a statuesque brunette with large brown eyes who'd edged her way into the group said. *Would she ever get a chance to sit?*

Marla mentally crossed her fingers this would be something she could answer truthfully. "And that would be ...?"

"Did you get to keep any of that gorgeous wardrobe?"

Yay! That one she could handle. "I did. My contract allowed me to keep two outfits each season."

The woman extended her hand. "I'm Liz Parsons. I live in the same building as Kitty on the first floor. What outfits did you choose?"

A detail woman. Fortunately, Marla could deal with this type of inquiry. "I wanted one of the evening gowns, a white silk, but those were too expensive. I mainly took some of the pantsuits, although I did select one dress, a wraparound green print number by Diane Von Furstenberg."

"I remember that one," Liz replied. "And the white silk evening gown, too. You wore that in the episode where you went underground to get the goods on a fake count."

She had? After a while, most of the scripts started sounding the same to Marla. "Good memory," she told the fashionista.

"That was the main reason I watched the show," Liz said. "The plots were good, and I usually was surprised when the killer was named, but your wardrobe was what brought me back each week."

Marla was just about to take a seat next to Kitty when her arm was grabbed by yet another admirer.

"Omigod! It's Letitia Carruthers, PI!" the arm-grabber cried.

"No!" her companion shouted. "It can't be."

"Kaitlin, this is my sister, Marla Dane," Kitty said, once again interceding. "She used to play Letitia Carruthers."

The arm-grabber, tall like Marla but with red hair and penetrating blue eyes, released her hold, reaching for Marla's hand instead. "I'm Kaitlin Fargo, Ms. Dane. Kitty has mentioned once or three thousand times that you were her sister, but we never thought we'd meet you."

"Nice to meet you, Kaitlin," Marla replied, still in her meet-the-public mode.

"You look different in person. Do you get that all the time?" Kaitlin asked.

A smiling skeptic. Marla came across one every so often. Their questions were a little too forward or a lot too personal. She reasoned that was the person's way of dealing with her celebrity. Though they probably didn't mean to offend, their comments were their way of cutting her down to their perceived size. She smiled again. "No, not everyone tells me I look different than I do on TV. Most realize a lot of makeup and costumes go into creating my character."

"Oh, sure," Kaitlin said, her tone less acerbic. "I didn't mean to insult you. I was just surprised to finally meet you in person."

"Not to worry," Marla replied. She offered her hand. "It's my pleasure to meet you, too."

Another woman stepped into view. "I guess I'm last to greet you, Letitia, uh, Marla. I'm Rita Haley. I live on the second floor of the building." She was a petite woman who appeared to be in her early sixties with fading brown hair and a smattering of freckles across her face.

"Nice to meet you, Rita," Marla said by rote. "With so many of you living in the building, why don't you just meet there?"

"Don't tell anyone," Sharee said, elbowing out Rita, "but sometimes the building seems to close in on us. This is our excuse to escape and have lunch together."

"But we do discuss books," Liz added.

"Along with other things," Sharee said, her sparkling brown eyes betraying their other agenda.

Scottie, apparently the leader for this session, spoke over the din of the other conversations. "Now that Marla has met you all, let's order so we can discuss this month's book."

"Oh, Scottie, couldn't we postpone the book this once?" Patty asked. "How often do we get to dine with a bona fide celebrity? Couldn't we use our discussion time to learn about her life in Hollywood instead?"

Scottie turned to Marla, her eyes both pleading and apologetic. "I don't think Marla came here to entertain us today."

"Oh, please say yes," Liz said, coaxing.

Marla exchanged a private look with her sister. As private as it could be with six other pairs of eyes on them.

Kitty attempted to come to her rescue. "C'mon, ladies. We can't put her on the spot like this. She's here today as a favor to me because I wanted to introduce her to some of my friends. She's not prepared to be grilled."

"If we promise to be good and not grill her?" Kaitlin asked, her voice sounding like a pleading child.

"You get to talk to her all the time," Patty said. "This could be our only chance."

"But …" Kitty tried to say.

This was insane. The last thing Marla wanted to do was be interviewed by her sister's friends. Although the media could go for the jugular at times, one came to accept that kind of behavior as par for the course in the entertainment world; that was their job, to angle for a great story. But these women were unpredictable. They might not realize their questions were inadvertently intrusive. Still, placating them seemed to be the only way she could sit down.

"It's okay, Kitty. Ladies, I'd be happy to answer a few questions, as long as you give me time to eat my lunch also," she told the group.

"Thank you, Marla," Scottie said. She directed her next comment to the rest of the group. "Okay, Marla has graciously agreed to answer a few questions. Let's limit them to one apiece."

three

. . .

And so it began. Although it had been a while since Marla fielded questions from a group of interviewers, the dance soon came back to her. She'd encountered most of their queries at one time or another in the past.

But previous interrogators had never been friends of her sister, the people who formed Kitty's support system. Marla told herself she needed to pay particular attention to these women who could make life difficult for Kitty if they felt short-changed.

Liz, apparently the resident fashionista given her earlier questions about the wardrobe Marla had been allowed to keep, went first. "Did you get along with everyone on the show?"

Marla had long ago learned the trick to responding to questions from those who didn't know her was to provide a safe answer while still giving the questioner a small nugget of new information. At least it would seem new to them. It rarely was. She just rearranged the words.

"The first season was a challenge as my recurring castmates and I got to know each other, especially Sebastian Collier, who played my friend on the police force. He'd been under the impression we shared lead status and grew a little testy after he learned that wasn't the case. He was ready to walk until the first reviews came in, praising the two of us for how well we worked together. Who could argue with such great publicity? He decided to stay on for the full season and, in the end, remained for all six seasons, even getting two Emmy nominations along the way."

Apparently her response satisfied Liz enough to turn over the role of inquisitor to Patty, her big fan.

"Have you ever dated anyone you worked with?" Patty asked. She offered a smug look to the rest of the group, apparently thinking she'd been first to ask the question that everyone else wanted to ask.

This one was easy. "I did once, and unlike most hookups within the industry which fail, this one worked. In fact, I married him. Carson Grant was the screenwriter for *Merrily and Company,* one of the first films I did after appearing on the stage in New York. We had a good marriage, although we tried never to be involved with the same project again to avoid potential problems working together. He passed away from pancreatic cancer during the second season of *On the Case.*" Over time it had become easier for her to talk about Hugo's death, but mentioning him still caused her voice to tremble slightly.

"Thank you for sharing that," Patty said.

"I appreciate your understanding how it's still somewhat difficult for me to talk about him," Marla replied. She hoped Hugo would understand how she fell back on her relationship with him when questions like this arose. It saved her from having to mention the few people connected with the show that she had seen socially, although not until the fifth season.

"I guess I'm next," Kaitlin said. Marla wondered if Kaitlin's grabbing her arm earlier would leave a bruise. "What was your favorite case?"

Once again, an old chestnut. She didn't have a favorite case. Truth be told, she could barely remember them from season to season—no fault of the writers or directors, who with the exception of just a few, made the show a quality production. But after the first year, the plotlines had begun to fuse together. Part of that was due to the formulaic approach the producers demanded, saying fans expected the show to be different every time but still predictable. To compensate for her foggy memory, she'd adopted three different cases and rotated which one she would cite each time this question arose. Which was almost every time.

"Let me think. If you are familiar with the show, you know that it is almost always Letitia who solves the case. Usually, she's not just the first to identify the culprit, but she does it against everyone else's opinion. I really like the scripts where her ideas are so far out, the viewer wonders how she'll ever dig out. For instance, in *Curse of the Unlucky Bride* the only clue that gave away the identity of the killer, one of her bridesmaids, was the poisoned flower that had been stuck in her bouquet, which only she touched."

Kaitlin nodded excitedly, her shoulder-length red bob swinging as she did. Until recently, when the gray had begun to invade Marla's lighter strawberry blond hair, Marla had considered going a darker red like Kaitlin, but her hairdresser on the set had discouraged her from going that direction, telling her the darker hue would wash out her complexion. "I remember that one. It was so unexpected because everyone else thought it was the groom's former fiancée. It certainly had me fooled."

They seemed to be going around the table, which helped avoid two or more asking a question at once. Next up: Sharee Cunningham, the neighbor on Kitty's floor. Marla doubted Kitty would ever need to borrow a cup of sugar from her – did people still do that? – but it would be good to have someone nearby she could go to if she or Kitty ever needed help.

"Were you ever hurt during a scene?" she asked.

Another oldie but goodie, because Marla had a pat response for this one too. "I'm happy to say, I've never received any broken bones or concussions on the show," she replied. "That's due in large part to the safety coordinators and stunt people. They did a wonderful job keeping me safe. The only mishap I experienced was slipping on wet grass on a hill while wearing wedgie shoes. I twisted my ankle pretty bad, but they were able to reblock my scenes so I could either sit or my feet wouldn't be showing."

"Did you ever have to use a real gun?" Rita Haley asked with so much interest, Marla wondered if the tiny woman had her own weapon.

"In the early years, on occasion, I carried a gun, but if I was forced to shoot anything, it was with fake bullets. However, even those situations can be problematic," Marla answered. "There's an armorer on-site at all times when a gun is involved. The producers tried to keep guns out of the mix. Whenever possible, Letitia used her head and not her gun."

They'd almost made it around the table. Only Scottie and Kitty remained.

"I'll pass for now," Kitty said.

"Guess that means I get the last question," Scottie said. "Have you met the new Letitia?

It wasn't the first time she'd been asked about her replacement, but it still took great effort to reply without sounding small.

"Yes, I met Julia Wainwright when she guest-starred on an episode during Season Five." She let it go at that. If pushed, she'd simply admit she hadn't spoken to the woman since then. She had no idea how Wainwright wound up in the role of

Younger Letitia, especially since she was at least three inches shorter than Marla with olive skin instead of Marla's peaches tone. Julia and one of the assistant producers had seemed chummy during her stint on the show. However, there'd been a complete turnover of production staff since then, so he probably had nothing to do with her being hired.

Scottie, a possible gossip columnist in the making, wasn't content to drop it there. "Just after the rehaul of the show was announced, I read where Julia Wainwright was asked if she thought she could fill your shoes. Her reply wasn't particularly flattering to you. She said something like, 'I don't think anyone could fill those size tens. I wear a size seven.' What was your reaction to that?"

Although Wainwright's reply hadn't been completely negative, she'd missed an opportunity to appear like she and Marla were fine with the changes. Deliberate? Marla had never been sure and in time had decided it wasn't worth pursuing. She began her response with a chuckle. "For starters, my shoe size is eight and a half. I think Julia was attempting to make a quip, that's all." She'd let this group decide what "attempting" meant.

Having taken her shot, Scottie tried to save Marla from further questions. "Okay, you all got a chance to quiz Marla. Let's move on to another topic."

"Don't be such a spoilsport, Scottie," Sharee replied. "Give us the scoop on your show, Marla." Marla vowed to be very careful with whatever she said to this one. "What really happened to make you walk? Just this one last question. I'm sure everyone here wants to know the story behind the headlines. We're Kitty's best friends. We'll keep whatever you tell us to ourselves."

"Right," Kaitlin cut in. "Just like you kept the amount of Rita's divorce settlement 'just between us' last winter."

Rita Haley shot a glance at Kaitlin. "Is that why I kept receiving so many calls from fundraisers?" she asked.

"C'mon, Rita, you made no secret of how much you took Bobby for," Kaitlin said in her own defense.

Sharee entered the fray. "You certainly didn't sit around bemoaning your new single status, either, Kaitlin."

"What do you mean by that, Sharee?" Kaitlin asked.

Called on her comment, Sharee sat back and studied her nails.

"Well?" Kaitlin prodded.

"I saw you running out to a car I didn't recognize," Sharee said finally. "I was sitting on my balcony at the time. One evening early in February."

"What were you doing on your balcony at that time of year?" Liz asked.

Sharee slid a not-so-appreciative glance Liz's way. "It was one of those days when the sun had come out and melted all the snow. I'd been cooped up so long, it was pleasant to sit out there as the day was ending and sip my sherry. So? Who was it, Kaitlin?"

"No big deal," Kaitlin replied in a lower voice. "I don't want to talk about it any more than Scottie wants to discuss what she's been up to."

"When I suggested we move on to another topic, I didn't mean we should turn on each other," Scottie said. "If Kaitlin wants to keep her love life private, I say we respect her wishes."

"Why did you call it my 'love life,' Scottie?" Kaitlin asked. "Sharee merely said she'd seen me get into an unknown car. Did you make that assumption because that's what's going on in your life?"

"Sorry, I must've misunderstood Sharee," Scottie responded. "Can we please find another topic to discuss? Maybe we should talk about the book after all."

"I hit a nerve, didn't I?" Kaitlin said, not ready to drop the topic at hand. "We all care about you, Scottie. Your social life has been more or less on hold since Wyatt died. We're happy for you, if you've started seeing someone."

Scottie telegraphed a "help me" look toward Kitty.

"Okay, okay, we all only want the best for Scottie, but if she doesn't want to talk about her private life, then we need to back off," Kitty said.

Marla was surprised by her sister coming to Scottie's aid. Knowing Kitty, she had to be as curious as the next person about their book club leader's life. But for some reason, in this instance, Kitty's sense of protectiveness outweighed her need to know.

Fortunately, their meals arrived. The next ten minutes were spent with everyone at the table making sure she'd received what she'd ordered, three of them asking for additional condiments, and one spilling a glass of water.

To Marla's relief, focused on their own foibles, the group never did get back to Scottie's question about the real reason Marla was no longer with the show.

"What was all that about?" Marla asked Kitty as they drove home from the restaurant.

"What? All their questions for you?"

"No, after that. The way they all seemed to come after each other. I detected more than one behind-the-scenes story going on with your friends. And it all has to do with who's seeing whom."

"Good way of putting it," Kitty replied from behind the wheel. "Only two of them, Patty and Liz, are married. Happily, for the most part. The others are either widowed, divorced or never married. With most of the group unattached, the herd grows anxious from time to time."

Marla attempted to put that statement into context with the scene she'd witnessed at the restaurant. "You mean, everyone is looking for a man?"

Kitty laughed. "God, no! At least not in the sense they all want to be married again. Most of them like their independence and don't want to give it up to a partner. But they're all still women with needs, both physical and emotional. And in some cases, financial."

"I got the impression they're all competing for the same men. That was the reason for the secrecy, so none of the others could cut into any one woman's relationships."

"I hear Letitia coming through in that statement," Kitty told her.

"No way! I was simply throwing out my own assessment of what I witnessed."

"Well, it's a pretty good summing up of all that craziness."

"I was surprised that you stayed out of the fray. And I was even more surprised when you stepped in to play peacemaker."

"Just between us? I didn't want the debate to extend to my own personal life. I'm not ready to talk about my relationship with Roger Halliwell. It may be over, but that wouldn't stop them from having a high old time discussing it. Plus, I sort of owed Scottie for rescuing you yesterday."

"Speaking of Scottie, is there something going on between the two of you?" Marla asked, deciding this was the time to learn what she could about the two women. Maybe it was why Tom Casey was worried about Kitty.

Kitty played dumb. "What do you mean? I told you why I came to her defense."

"Just before you did, she sent you a look I couldn't decipher. A look that seemed to say, 'I won't tell if you don't tell.' Did I interpret correctly?"

"I thought you said Letitia was behind you now. Why are you pushing this?"

"I'm not Letitia, but I am your sister. I'd think you'd want me to know if something was troubling you."

"Does the same go for you, not-Letitia?"

Damn! She'd gone too far and now had her own privacy to protect. "What are you saying, Kitty?"

"You know very well what I meant, but on the one percent chance my intent is still cloudy, what I was getting at is the unfinished business you've left behind in La La Land. You've only revealed a fraction of what happened back there and what I'm guessing is still going on. I assume you have your reasons for leaving me out of whatever brought you back to Minnesota, and for now I'm respecting that. But sooner or later, you'll have to come clean with me if you ever hope to resolve those issues."

Despite appearing to be a bit of a ditz at times, Kitty was pretty sharp when it came to reading Marla. Maybe her sister could help her get beyond the mess she'd made, but Marla wasn't ready to lay all that on her now. She needed more time to think through her options.

KITTY LET the next two days pass without pushing Marla to join her in more of her current activities, sparing her learning the tango at a ballroom dance class and painting a pitcher in Kitty's ceramics class. She hadn't gone far because the community room at Rambling Meadows accommodated a myriad of offerings. Other undertakings like horticulture were offered in the greenhouse and other outbuildings behind the complex owned by the Rambling Family that condo residents were allowed to use.

Marla used Kitty's absences to settle into her room, order out for her special comfort food - seedless white grapes, chips and French onion dip - and schedule a massage at a nearby spa.

The quiet time was a godsend. Many diverse and difficult thoughts had bombarded her lately. To get past licking her wounds, she needed to sort them out and rid herself of as many nonessentials as she could. In a way, the book club encounter had served as a diversion, which she needed right then. But now she had to focus on where she was headed the rest of her life.

She also checked in with both her manager, Jayne Yarmouth, and her agent, Deidre Mansfield. Jayne was the one who'd counseled her to get away from the LA scene for a while. Deidre, who should've been busy finding her new projects the last few months, had conveniently gone AWOL. She probably should be fired, but Marla sensed that's what Deidre wanted, and she didn't plan to give in to her. She half suspected Deidre knew about the producers' plan to replace her long before she knew.

Kitty returned a little after two. "Why are the police here? A van marked Crime Scene Unit, which I saw when I left, is still parked out front. The army of technicians in blue onesies is gone, but they left behind that telltale yellow tape."

"What? Police were on the premises? I had no idea." She hadn't gone near the balcony all day or she might have seen what was happening.

"Sounds like I need to do some reconnaissance around the building," Kitty said, heading for the door. "I'll start next door with Tom Casey."

Her hand barely touched the doorknob when knocking sounded on the other side.

Must be someone who lived in the building; an outsider would've had to ring for entrance.

Marla opened the door, and Scottie rushed in. "They think I did it," she announced dramatically as she flounced around the room. "Me. I'd never hurt a fly."

"Come sit down and tell us what has you so worked up," Marla said, gently guiding the woman to the sofa.

Though she sat, Scottie shook her head back and forth as if

that action would make whatever had happened go away. "It's Drake," she managed to get out, her voice more a cry.

"Drake?" Marla asked, trying to recall if she'd met someone by that name yet.

"Elliot," Scottie mumbled. "Drake Elliot. He's dead."

four

. . .

"**D**rake Elliot is dead?" Kitty said, dropping into the closest chair.

Scottie didn't/couldn't answer, having launched into a crying jag.

"Get her some water, Kitty," Marla directed while she settled next to Scottie and rubbed her shoulders. "Go ahead, Scottie. Get it out of your system so you can tell us what's going on." She cooed her words like one would settle a sobbing child.

Kitty dragged herself from the chair and headed to the kitchen, still gaping at her distressed friend.

Scottie continued blubbering even after Kitty arrived with the water. Finally, after another few minutes, their visitor, her entire face red from crying, reached for the tissues Kitty had thought to bring. She dabbed her eyes and blew her nose.

"I'm sorry. I shouldn't have gone on so, but this is so beyond anything I've ever experienced. I held it in as best I could while the police questioned me, but once I got here, I let go."

"A man, this Drake Elliot, is dead, and the police have already interviewed you?" Marla asked, attempting to understand.

"Yes, they came to my place about an hour ago. At first, I thought I was under arrest, but they said it was too early yet to accuse anyone. But from the questions they asked and all the information they seemed to already know about Drake and me, even I thought I might be guilty as their interrogation progressed. But I'm not. I may have discovered he was the scum of the earth, but I'd never ..."

Marla exchanged a glance with Kitty, who simply shrugged. Kitty must know more than she was letting on.

"Let's start at the beginning," Marla said, since Kitty apparently wasn't ready to probe deeper. "Who is, was, Drake Elliot?"

"He claimed he was a retired stockbroker who still dabbled in various venture capital opportunities," Scottie began. "He moved into the building sometime this past year. I met him several months ago at someone's cocktail party, but it's only been recently that I, we, started seeing each other."

"Seeing, as in dating?" Kitty asked.

"Okay, you could call it that."

"You mean you ...?" Kitty asked, her voice rising.

"Don't sound so judgmental, Kitty," their visitor replied. "We both know about your track record."

Though not surprised by this accusation, given the looks the two women had exchanged earlier in the week, Marla forced herself not to look at her sister. Plenty of time to pursue that comment later.

"Is that what Kaitlin was getting at the other day when she referred to your recent love life?" Marla asked.

Scottie sucked in her lips. She obviously didn't want to get into this despite the fact that she'd started it. She blew out a breath. "I guess it's all going to come out soon enough anyway. You might as well know now. I ran into him again about six weeks ago and he started calling me and asking me out to dinner. It seemed harmless enough, and I really haven't dated much since my husband died.

"He preferred to pick me up at the front entrance rather than come to my door. I dismissed it as his being a very private man. I knew he wasn't married; at least he lived alone here in the building.

"Dining out led to a few overnights at different motels. None here in Maple Knolls. I liked the intrigue. My life had become so predictable until I started seeing him. He offered something I hadn't been getting. Okay, sex, but the mystique too."

"How did it go from the intrigue to your now calling him the scum of the earth?" Marla asked.

Scottie paused long enough to take a breath. "Two things. Early on, he'd describe some of the financial deals he had in the works. I acted interested because that's what you do when you're just getting to know someone. Not that I really cared about investing. As time went by, his references to his deals became more frequent until about two and a half weeks ago he came right out and asked if I'd like to go in on this 'sure thing' he had going. I shut him down right away, although I thought he'd just been asking to be polite.

"He tried one more time two days later, and when I made it clear I wasn't interested, he ended the evening there and then. He was never particularly threatening, but once it was clear I wasn't giving him any money, he dropped me just like that."

Marla had remained quiet throughout Scottie's dissertation. This story sounded all too familiar to her, and not because it had been the plot of one Letitia's cases. For now, she had to shut her own recent history out of her mind. This was Scottie's story, and she needed their full attention.

"Apparently he was murdered," Marla said. "What do you know about that?"

"The police didn't tell me much except that his body was

found at the edge of the pond in front of the building. He suffered some sort of head injury, but they didn't specify."

"That pond is directly in front of part of the building," Kitty said. "Surely someone saw what happened from their balcony."

"Not in the wee hours of the morning," Scottie replied. "They wouldn't give me an exact time of death, but they asked me where I was from ten to six this morning."

"Why do they think you might have something to do with his murder?" Marla asked.

"They wouldn't say, but they knew I'd been with him recently. They were hoping I could shed some light on his life of late."

"What did you tell them?" Marla asked.

"I tried to limit my responses to our dating, but they already knew we hadn't parted amicably."

Marla got the distinct impression Scottie had skipped over something. "Why was that?"

Scottie began to wring her hands. "I didn't exactly say, 'no, thank you,' on that final date when he pushed for me to invest. I, uh, blew up. In the restaurant. I told him exactly what he could do with his investment. In front of the other diners and the staff. He simply walked out, leaving me there with the bill while everyone continued to sneak looks at me."

"That must have been very humiliating," Kitty said, becoming empathetic.

"At first, but the longer I sat there, I realized how speaking my mind for once had been so freeing. Since I was paying for both dinners, I lingered long enough to toast my good fortune with the expensive wine he'd ordered and then went home via rideshare."

"That's how the police tracked you down?" Kitty asked.

"How would they have known to start with the restaurant, if Scottie paid for the meal?" Marla asked Kitty.

"Drake apparently ate there frequently. All the staff knew him," Scottie replied. "If the police checked his charge accounts, they would've come across prior dinners when he did pay."

"Makes sense," Marla said.

Kitty edged in closer, taking the chair just next to where Scottie sat with Marla on the sofa. "What about ... you know ... the sex part?"

Leave it to her sister to have zeroed in on that aspect of Scottie's story.

"At first, they attempted to address that part in general terms. So I answered that way. Apparently they wanted more specific details from me because they came right out and asked if we'd had sex. When I told them yes, they wanted to know how often. At that point, I drew the line, although when they continued to push, I admitted to more than twice and less than ten times."

All they'd have to do was check Elliot's motel bill charge records to discover the number of times they'd spent the night, or part of it, together, although such records wouldn't indicate the number of times per night they'd been intimate.

None of them spoke for several beats. Marla and Kitty seemed to have run out of questions, and Scottie had stopped crying. What more was there to do, unless the police returned and did arrest their friend?

Kitty was the first to break the silence. "It sounds like so far you're in the clear, but just as a precaution, maybe you should find yourself an attorney."

"I already have a call in to a friend asking her for a reference. But that's not why I'm here."

"You didn't just want to bring us up to speed?" Kitty asked.

Scottie twisted around to face Marla. "No. I'm here for you, Let— Marla. I need your help."

"My help?" Marla asked, caught off guard.

"Help me learn who killed Drake."

"Me? Why me?" Marla asked.

"You've been around more murders than me."

Marla's stomach dipped the same way it did when she forgot her lines. Surely Scottie wasn't going there. "You do realize those were scripted murders. Fiction, Scottie. Make-believe. I solved them in an hour's time every week. I have no more experience investigating real-life murders than you or Kitty."

Scottie took her hand. "I know that, Marla. I know you're not Letitia Carruthers. But surely some of those procedures and techniques rubbed off on you after six years? Consider the questions you've asked me already. Where did those come from if they weren't embedded somewhere in your subconscious?"

"I was just being logical as I tried to get you to calm down and tell us what happened. Kitty questioned you, too."

Scottie's eyes resembled those of a puppy shut out in the rain. "Please, Marla. I could find a bona fide professional to take on my case, but that would take time, and I got the impression the police are under the gun to solve this quickly, whether they find the real killer or not. I don't want them to land on me."

"A good attorney will help you with that," Marla said.

"True, with the legal things. But I need someone with a legitimate reason to mingle with the residents here in the building and ask questions the police won't even think to ask. That's you. You're new, and you're a celebrity. No one else I know can claim that distinction."

Marla was taken aback with Scottie's read on her situation. She'd come up with one reason why she should "investigate" this murder that Marla never would have considered. "That suggests you think someone who lives here is the killer. Because his body was found on this property?"

Her question brought Kitty to her feet. "That's crazy. The people who live here might appear to be slightly unusual, but they're not killers."

"The police think I am," Scottie said.

Marla debated how far they should let Scottie go with this idea. If the woman truly believed she was the top suspect, maybe she'd start acting like she was whether she intended to or not. "You don't know that for sure, Scottie. If you're that concerned, follow through on getting someone to represent you to have in the bullpen in case you need a lawyer. Beyond that, act like the innocent person you are."

Scottie's chin jutted out a tad more. "Sound advice. I'll try to follow it. But I'll only be able to relax and convince everyone I am innocent if I know someone else is working behind the scenes to make sure I stay that way."

"But Scottie ..." Marla started to say until she was cut off.

"Would it sweeten the pot any if I told you I have a few friends in the entertainment business? Friends in the know about movie and TV deals in the works."

Dear, sweet, possible killer Scottie had connections?

How had she landed on the one carrot that might get Marla's attention? What had Kitty told her about Marla's recent setbacks?

Would it be so bad to mimic her alter ego this one last time if it meant clearing Scottie's name, particularly since she could relate to Scottie's situation more than Scottie or Kitty knew and that she wanted them to know? And maybe Scottie could find a new lead that would take her back to Hollywood, although if she'd learned anything in the last several months, it was not to count on the good intentions of friends. Even well-meaning ones.

"I'll see what I can find out," Marla said. "I'm not saying I'll investigate. I'll just talk to a few people to learn whatever I can about Drake Elliot."

Scottie threw her arms around her in an exuberant embrace.

"Thank you, thank you, thank you. I'll call my friend even if you don't uncover anything."

"Just as long as you remember I'm not trained in this area. I'm not promising anything."

"Got it," Scottie replied, jumping up and racing for the door.

Another thought occurred to Marla. "One more thing, and this is critical, Scottie. This is just between you, Kitty and me. And your attorney, if you get one."

five

. . .

itty stared at Marla dumbfounded. "Were you serious about turning into a real PI?" she asked incredulously.

"I said I'd look into things. I tried to make it clear I wouldn't investigate. I'm no longer Letitia Carruthers."

"Good luck making that distinction clear to Scottie. All she heard from you was yes."

Kitty had voiced Marla's fear. But she hadn't had much choice, given Scottie's heightened state of desperation. "Then I'll have to keep reminding her."

Kitty appeared to accept that statement. "What do you want me to do?"

Should she be concerned her sister was a little too enthusiastic about being so close to a murder? "Thanks for the offer, but for now, just be willing to consult with me when I need another set of ears." Another thought occurred to her. "Unless you ever ran into Drake Elliot?"

Kitty swiveled around and skittered off to the kitchen.

Had she hit a nerve? She'd better find out now before she got too far nosing around the other building residents.

She followed her sister to the kitchen. "You didn't answer my question."

Kitty conveniently had her head in the fridge. "What would you like for dinner? I've got several frozen options from that restaurant we went to the other day."

Kitty's non-answer was even more curious. "Kitty? What aren't you telling me about the man?"

Kitty closed the refrigerator door and slumped onto one of the barstools at the island. "I know who he was. A good-looking single man does not escape anyone's attention in this condo complex for long. I may have been at that same cocktail party Scottie mentioned. It was several months ago anyhow. I asked someone who he was, and when I heard he was an eligible bachelor, I found some excuse to approach him and introduce myself."

"Do social events like that happen often around here?" Marla asked.

Kitty raised her shoulders in a shrug. "That depends on your definition of 'often.' There's at least one complex-sponsored social event each month. Not everyone attends them, but those who do are a mix of the singles and couples. The singles include several widows and a few older, unmarried women. Some of the singles prefer gatherings with other singles like themselves. You get the picture."

"Sort of like hunting grounds?" Marla said.

"Crude, but one way of putting it."

"Would it be safe to say these singles parties aren't publicized or discussed with anyone who isn't single?"

"Uh, yeah."

Marla thought back over the social events she'd been invited to in LA in the last few years. Not so many in the last six months; she'd become a bit of a pariah since being dropped from the show. But before that she received more invites than she could ever accept. Hostesses spent hours curating their invitation lists to ensure only the "right" mix of guests would be invited, and her name had usually been included. Although hookups occasionally resulted from these parties, most guests were more interested in being seen or making connections for their next project.

Discovering how the singles-only parties in the complex worked might be very helpful. Not that she was interested in finding a soulmate at this time in her life. She'd had that with Hugo. It was too much to hope she'd ever find that kind of relationship again. But since she was single and new to the building, what better place to begin her digging?

But her first stop was Tom Casey ten minutes later. He hadn't approached Marla since she arrived. Curious, since she was here thanks to him. Before she "looked into" the murder of Drake Elliot, she wanted to know what was going on with her sister.

"Come in, come in," Tom said after she knocked on his door.

Her first impression of Tom Casey was that of a slightly overweight basset hound with red hair tinged with gray. Adorable but not particularly handsome. "I'm Marla Dane, Tom. We haven't met in person even though we've spoken on the phone."

She took a seat on a sofa facing a similar piece on which he lighted. "Thanks for taking my concerns about Kitty seriously and coming back to Minnesota," he told her. "Have you had a chance to observe her erratic behavior?"

She hadn't made much progress in that department yet. "Early days, Tom. The one thing I have observed is the almost frenetic pace at which Kitty is engaging in outside activities."

"That's just surface stuff, symbolic of whatever's going on inside her head and heart."

"What is going on inside my sister?" she asked.

He rubbed the back of his neck before replying. "I don't know, Marla. That's why I begged you to come visit her. All I can do is describe some of the recent comments and actions that haven't seemed like Kitty."

"Tell me about those and let me judge for myself."

He folded his hands and momentarily brought them to his face. "Even in the short time you've been here, you've probably noticed how her days and nights are a constant stream of activities. As long as I've known her, she's always kept herself busy, but of late it's been like she doesn't know what to do with her down time."

"Yes, I've noticed. I thought that was because she's wanted to keep me busy to take my mind off the difficulties I've had in LA."

"That makes a certain amount of sense, but have you gotten involved?"

"I attended her book club earlier in the week, but that's all. I told her I just wanted to relax and regroup, and so far, she's respected my wishes. What else have you noticed?"

"Have you checked out her wardrobe?"

"She's always liked clothes. And shoes," Marla replied.

"And has she always worn form-fitting pants? Low-cut sweaters. Stiletto heels?"

She thought back over the types of clothes she'd seen Kitty wear over the years. There was no denying her sister liked being on the cutting edge of fashion trends. But had she turned up the heat on those choices?

"I hate to admit it, Tom, but I've been so into my own head since I've arrived, I haven't really noticed Kitty's wardrobe choices. But now that I'm aware of your observations, I'll be on the alert."

He nodded. "Good! I'm not known for my knowledge of women's fashion. I'm glad you've joined that team."

"Have you noticed anything else?" she asked.

His gaze wandered around the room a few beats before returning to look at her. "Kitty has never been shy around the opposite sex. But lately it's been like she's on some kind of constant aphrodisiac where men are concerned. Most men. Not me. She's never seen me as a romantic partner." His voice dropped off with that last admission, regret underlying his tone.

Roger Halliwell's name came immediately to mind. Kitty had been so intent on spending time with him in his boat, she'd missed picking Marla up at the airport. Possibly, Kitty had been involved with Drake Elliot, even though she'd denied having dated him. Maybe there'd even been something between her and Rex Alcorn, the way the two interacted with each other when he'd let her into Kitty's condo.

"Kitty's been divorced five years. She has every right to see men socially."

"Of course she does," he said. "What I'm talking about is a matter of degree."

"Are you saying she's become a sexaholic?" Marla asked.

"I wouldn't go that far," he replied, "although I'd have to check out a definition of a sexaholic first, if there is such a thing. She just seems so frantic about her need to be with a man."

"Where did you get that impression?"

He pursed his lips briefly. "It's like I've become her best girl-friend. She feels comfortable sharing things with me. Things I've never asked about." He paused. "I'm not gay, Marla. I'm a straight man with needs of my own. I'd rather not be subjected to her chattiness."

Talk about oversharing. Marla hadn't expected to hear so much about Tom's personal lifestyle. "Do those needs include my sister?"

He didn't reply at once. He seemed to be giving her question lots of thought. "She's never been interested in me," he said at length. "How I feel about her doesn't matter."

"Have you ever told her?" she couldn't help asking.

"I've come close more than once, but I'm not in her league. Why embarrass us both with her rejection?"

Tom Casey had it bad for her sister. That should've been clear from his plaintive phone call when Marla was still back in LA, but it didn't register until that moment. Most likely, something really was going on with Kitty, but it was being interpreted and now described to her by this infatuated man. How much could she trust his judgment?

"Busyness, sexy clothes and accelerated interest in men," she said, summarizing what he'd told her. "I'll watch for those, but then what? Any ideas?"

He shrugged. "I don't know. That's why I asked you to come. You know your sister better than I. But like I said before, these are outward signs of something going on inside her. You have to figure out what it is and then help her deal with it."

"Is that all?" She didn't mean to belittle him, but damn, that was a big order, especially now that she'd agreed to look into the Elliot murder for Scottie Richards.

He hung his head. "Yeah. Big assignment. But she's worth the trouble."

"You've given me a lot to think about. I'll be back when I have a plan."

"Please, don't tell her that I've shared my feelings about her with you."

Time to move on to her other assignment. "Actually, I stopped by for another reason."

He cocked his head, apparently not expecting more. "Okay? How can I help you?"

"I assume you've heard about the murder of one of the complex's residents, Drake Elliot?"

"Who hasn't? It was the topic of coffee hour this morning. Weekday mornings, a group of us guys get together at that little grocery store down the road. They have a small café and the best coffee around. Anyway, Jim Purvis had been out walking his dog about seven this morning when he saw first one and then several police cars barrel into the parking lot out front. They wouldn't let him get closer than a hundred feet from where they were swarming, but he managed to gather the major gist of what had happened."

"I understand the victim, Elliot, had a condo here in the building?"

"Moved in sometime in the last year," he replied.

"What do you know about him?"

Tom scratched his jaw. "Curious question. Don't you want to know more about the murder?"

"You'd think so, but the thing is the police have already visited at least one of our fellow condo owners, and she thinks they were paying her more than passing attention. I agreed to nose around a bit and see if she has reason to be concerned."

Tom lifted a brow. "They'd only have reason to pay attention to her if she was somehow involved."

"That sounds quite reasonable to you and me, but we weren't seeing him socially the past few months."

"Oh. Wow." He scrunched up his face, apparently processing what she'd just revealed. "Funny, I don't recall hearing any scuttlebutt about his love life since he moved in. Seemed a little strange since the guy was the type who would've appealed to the manhunters around here. I rarely ran into him, so I haven't thought much more about him since I first met him at some party."

"I should mention that anything I tell you or that we discuss from here on is confidential. Is that okay with you?

"Uh, sure. I guess. How did you get involved in all this? You haven't even been here a week." Then he blinked, a light coming on in his eyes. "Wait. Surely you don't think you can play Letitia Carruthers, PI, here in Minnesota?"

She waved off his question. "No, no. If anyone is aware how much I'm no longer the great detective, it's me. But convincing the crowd around here is another story. All I plan to do is ask a few questions. The kind a visitor might ask."

"Is Kitty involved in this?" he asked, worry underlying his tone.

"She knows about it, and I've told her I didn't need her help," Marla replied a little too fast.

Tom nodded. "You may have said as much to her, but don't assume that was enough to keep her uninvolved."

She laughed, hopefully dismissing his concern, although she still had qualms herself. "Thanks for the warning. But let's forget about Kitty for now. Tell me what else you know about Elliot."

"Nothing else. Didn't have much to do with the guy and don't know of any gossip about him."

She sank into the sofa cushions. "You disappoint me. I was under the impression you knew a little something about everyone in this building. Kitty told me you were on the social committee."

He snorted. "Dear Marla, the first thing you need to learn in your investigation is that there's the social committee and then there's the underground singles alliance. My name for the latter."

"Sounds like you're not a fan of that group? Too much competition with your committee?"

"Don't I wish. No, apparently the events my group organizes are too tame for the singles who are out to end that status."

"Tame? Sounds rather kinky. Is it? Don't you attend their events? You're a single, aren't you?"

"Widower the last ten years. I went to one or two a while back out of curiosity to learn what my committee wasn't offering."

"And?"

"Mainly they sorted out the singles from the couples and older people who attend events held by the social committee. Other than that difference, those gatherings were pretty tame themselves. Most of the singles in this building are over forty-five. More likely, they're in their late fifties and early sixties. Younger singles tend to gravitate to the apartments on the other side of town."

"What about the guys you said you have coffee with? Has anyone there ever talked about Drake Elliot?"

"Not very often." He stopped. Rubbed his jaw again. "There was some discussion about him when he first moved in, but that was months ago. I'm not sure I can remember what was said."

"Try. It could be important."

He closed his eyes and made several faces as he apparently attempted to recall what he'd heard months before. He suddenly blinked his eyes open. "One of the guys, Jim Purvis, I think, the guy who found the body, said he mentioned something about investments. Not his current portfolio. We all talk about those. Several think they're amateur day traders." He shook his head. "No, it wasn't about our stuff. Gimme another minute. It's starting to come back to me."

Marla attempted to wait as patiently as possible. She sensed Tom knew more than he realized.

"Oh, yes. Now I remember. A chance to buy in. But Jim was sharp enough to recognize that supposed casual reference to this deal for what it was, a hook."

"I take it he didn't jump?" she asked.

"Jim told us he didn't outright turn down Elliot. He dismissed it, acted like it was some pipe dream of Elliot's and he was blowing smoke. And Elliot was shrewd enough to let it go, although Jim didn't see the man in the fitness room again."

"What about Elliot and the ladies, the ladies in the building? Did you pick up on any intel about that?"

"Early on, some of the guys asked if any of the rest of us had met the new guy in town. All four of them except me had run into him one way or another. The general consensus was that he was definitely competition for the single ladies in the complex and to keep our distance from him because he seemed to be some sort of wolf in sheep's clothing."

"What do you mean by that?"

"He seemed on the up-and-up, but Jim suspected he could be trouble if he continued to hit up other residents about his investment opportunities as he had him."

"Thanks. That was a big help."

"Yeah? Sounds like you know something more. Gonna share?"

"I'm not at liberty to reveal very much at this time, but let's just say your coffee pals seem to have been right on the mark."

Deep lines furrowed the bridge of his nose. "Then his murder somehow involved money?"

"I don't know for sure, but it looks like it."

"Be careful, Marla," he said, his tone becoming even more serious. "I'm sure you already know this, but what you're getting yourself into isn't one of your weekly crimes you can solve in an hour."

"I'm well aware of that, but I'll be extra careful now that you've warned me."

"And Marla? I'm always here if you need more information or just a hand to hold."

six

. . .

$\mathcal{M}$arla returned to Kitty's condo and went directly to the fridge and opened a can of Diet Coke. She hoped the caffeine would sharpen her brain as she processed what she'd learned so far about Drake Elliot from Scottie and Tom Casey.

"If your bad habits are the same as the old days, you've got a lot on your mind and are relying on that beverage to help you think," Kitty said from the kitchen entrance.

"Wouldn't you say Scottie's case qualifies?"

Kitty was about to let it go when another thought hit her. "But you were drinking it *before* Scottie came calling. Something else is troubling you. Out with it, sis."

Sometimes her sister could be right on point when it came to reading her. But that didn't mean she had to respond. "Let's save that discussion for another day. Right now, my brain has enough to contend with trying to find out who killed Drake Elliot. I just talked to Tom Casey."

"And?"

"And he was somewhat helpful. I got his take on as much as he could remember hearing about Elliot per the impressions of the guys in his coffee klatch. Although it appeared to echo what Scottie told us about being approached to invest in some project, he didn't shed any more details on what we already knew." She didn't mention Tom's warning to be careful. It didn't take much to trigger Kitty's imagination.

"You should probably talk to Rex Alcorn," Kitty said.

Rex? Not that guy. "Why him?"

"Rex knows everything that goes on in this building."

That was a surprise. When he'd come to her rescue letting her into Kitty's condo, he gave the impression of wanting to leave as soon as he could escape. "He seemed so taciturn when I met him."

"He was a police officer for years. It was his job to observe."

Marla set down the can. "I heard something to that effect from Scottie when she let me into the building, but I didn't think much of it at the time. It doesn't surprise me he was a cop even though he didn't say he was."

"He doesn't advertise it. He told me once he learns more that way."

"What do you think he'd say about my agreeing to look into this murder?"

Kitty considered. "He'd probably advise against proceeding further."

Rather diplomatic for Kitty. "Why didn't Scottie go to him instead of me?"

Kitty leaned in and took a sip from Marla's can. "With his police background, she was probably worried he'd advise going to them."

Marla filed away that tidbit.

"Given that, I'll skip talking with Rex for now. Maybe if I need to run something by him, I'll ask for his advice."

"If not Rex, who do you plan to interview next?" Kitty asked.

"Who would you suggest?"

"As it just so happens, there's a wine and cheese party tomorrow night for the singles crowd in the building. I could get us an invite if you want?"

Tom Casey hadn't mentioned anything about a wine and cheese party. "Will it be a repeat of the book club, where I get bombarded with questions about Letitia?"

"Maybe. A little. Although some of the women who'll be there were at the book club lunch and already got their chance to question you. As for the guys, I couldn't begin to predict how they'll react. But it's the best option I can come up with right now."

Marla had managed to get through the bombardment of questions at the book club lunch, but she needed more ammunition when she faced this larger group.

"At least you won't have to address the whole group at once," Kitty said. "You can decide which individuals you want to zero in on and move from person to person."

"Okay, that's good news," Marla replied, debating how she could make the most of these small group settings.

Kitty went off to shower and change for dinner with a friend. Most likely a male friend, but Marla didn't ask. Instead, she turned her attention to what she'd wear to the party the next night. Probably not necessary, but making the right impression the first- time meeting some of these folks could enhance the quality of information she could glean from them.

She'd narrowed her choices down to a brown jersey sheath and a silver-gray pantsuit when Kitty entered with her phone in hand. "It's for you. It's Patty Goodhue. She didn't have your number." She handed her phone to Marla and moved two feet to the side.

Patty Goodhue? Wasn't she one of the women at the book club lunch? Which one? She couldn't recall. "Hello?"

"Let— Marla, thanks for taking my call. Do you have dinner

plans tonight? You didn't get much to eat the other day what with all of us so interested in your life in Hollywood. I'd like to treat you to dinner at one of my favorite restaurants to make up for it. Sorry for the late invite. Please say yes. I promise I'll put my fangirl questions aside."

Kitty, who could hear everything Patty said, had a funny expression on her face. Something between surprise and concern. Marla quickly thought through the possible reasons she could give for turning down the invitation. Then it occurred to her that maybe Patty might know something about Drake Elliot. "Okay," she said before she changed her mind.

She didn't dare glance at Kitty, who pounced as soon as Marla returned her phone. "Why did you say yes? Didn't you see my face and my head shaking?"

"You're the one who's been encouraging me to get out and meet people. What's wrong with Patty Goodhue?"

Kitty released a breath. "What's wrong with her? You tell me what's wrong with having dinner with the wife of the chief of police."

Marla sat down on the bed. "Police chief, as in the same folks who're investigating the murder?"

"The one and the same," Kitty replied.

"Do you think her invitation is connected to the case? Surely police chiefs don't send their wives out to dinner to investigate potential suspects. Plus, I'm not a suspect. I never met the man."

"No, of course not. But I don't think it's a coincidence. Be careful with what you tell her, and especially don't mention what you promised Scottie. Or anything about Scottie."

"No, I won't."

She had to keep reminding herself of that pledge as she dined with Patty.

She didn't remember who Patty was until the woman picked her up at the building entrance at her favorite portico. Patty was the first woman she met at the luncheon. The one with the ash-blond ponytail who had started gushing the moment Marla arrived. Her hair was drawn back in a loose bun this evening.

"I appreciate your accepting my late-notice invitation," she told Marla later at the restaurant as they eyed their menus.

"I appreciate your thinking of me," Marla replied, trying to keep her response general.

"I told you the other day that you did so much as Letitia to help me as a woman over fifty. Which was true, although I didn't say why."

Marla waved it away. "Not necessary."

"Oh, but it is. You see, I was widowed in my late thirties with two young children to raise. I'd worked as a teaching assistant before I was married but quit once the children arrived. My husband had provided well for us, both in life and in death. It's not like I had to work, but I had to learn how to deal with our finances overnight. It was overpowering. Quite a struggle. I had the kids to keep me going until they got older, and then suddenly it was just me.

"I floundered a bit until about six years ago when I started watching your show. It spoke to me. I'm a little bit younger than you but not by much. I realized I needed something more in my life. Something exciting. That turned out to be working as an administrative assistant to a lieutenant with the St. Paul police department. My boss was Colman Goodhue—newly divorced Colman Goodhue—and despite what they tell you and caution about office romances, I fell hard for him. And it was mutual.

"During that time, I continued to watch your show. I couldn't stop talking about it. I told him how it had brought me out of a multiyear funk, and that got him watching it. It didn't take long for him to become a fan as well."

It never failed to surprise her when viewers told her how the show had affected them personally, even though that was one of her driving goals an actress. The setbacks of the last several months aside, admissions like this were powerful stuff that shouldn't be taken lightly. When Patty stopped and there was a lull in the conversation, Marla felt compelled to say something. "Thank you for telling me that, Patty. I still appreciate hearing how Letitia impacted people's lives."

Patty put down her menu and gazed directly at her. "I have something to confess. I invited you to join me for another reason."

Uh-oh. She wanted help contacting someone in LA. It didn't happen often, but that kind of request arose on occasion. Marla had developed a standard reply. "Oh? What would that be?"

"My husband wants to join us." She stared down at her clasped hands. "He works for the Maple Knolls police department. In fact, he's the chief."

Might as well cut to the chase. "Is this about the murder of Drake Elliot?"

Patty had the grace to blink. "You, uh, already know about that. Of course, news like murder can sweep quickly through a residential building like yours." She held up a hand. "Please don't be alarmed. You're not a suspect or anything like that."

Marla wasn't alarmed. And at this point, she wasn't even angry to be dining under questionable circumstances. Mainly, she was curious. "Why does he want to see me?"

"I can answer that question myself," said a male voice just behind Marla. He moved to stand to the side of Patty so Marla could see him. He appeared to be a little under six feet, short reddish hair going gray with a paunch in the making. "I'm Colman Goodhue, Ms. Dane," he said, extending his hand.

"Chief Goodhue," Marla returned, taking his hand. "Please be seated. I'm curious to hear what's on your mind."

"I apologize for getting you here like this," he said as soon as he was in his seat. "I didn't want to alarm you by asking you to meet me at the station house, and I wasn't ready to show up at your condo complex."

"Okay, so much for the amenities. What's on your mind?" She could almost hear Letitia in her words.

"I'm new to this job, Ms. Dane. I came from the St. Paul police department where I worked robbery and vice all my career except for early days in traffic management. Although I attained detective status, I never was involved with a homicide. And Maple Knolls hasn't experienced a homicide in over ten years." He sat back and eyed her. "In other words, none of us on the force have much experience finding killers."

"But I heard someone from your department has already questioned at least one of the residents in my building, and that was the result of reviewing the victim's credit card charges and tracking down witnesses who had seen Mr. Elliot recently." The words were out before she realized how much she'd revealed despite her promise to Kitty.

He raised a brow. "Ah. So you're pretty much up to speed with where things stand. Good. I won't have to go through preliminaries." He leaned forward. "Here's the thing. Patty has been one of your devoted fans for years. She's the one who got me watching your show. It offered me something I wasn't getting in my job, investigating murders."

She started to remind him that the woman she portrayed was pure fiction but stopped. He knew that. And yet he still wanted to talk to her. Why?

"You're probably asking yourself why I've turned to you instead of asking for help from one or more of the larger police departments in the area or even the state patrol," he said. "I could and probably should do that, and that remains an option if you turn me down."

"Turn you down?" she asked.

"I may not have any direct experience investigating murders, but I consider myself a logical man, and my logic tells me there's a link between this man's murder and something or someone in your condo building. I need an unbiased pair of eyes and ears on the inside."

"I presume you mean me?" she asked, attempting to keep her tone devoid of emotion.

"Uh, yes." He paused. "Now before you remind me you were just an actress reading your lines and that you're not a real investigator, let me assure you I'm well aware of that. It's the fact that you're accustomed to being scripted plus the fact that you're now an insider in that complex that makes you the ideal person to do this."

This was incredible. He'd just described almost the same task Scottie had charged her with, except Scottie's reason was to protect herself. Colman Goodhue's reason was to protect his job and his department. The difference was that she could tell Scottie at any time that she wanted out because she was getting nowhere. Could she ask Goodhue for the same type of out?

"You're not saying anything, Ms. Dane. Have I completely lost you or angered you?"

"Call me Marla, and no, you've done neither. I'm just surprised to be asked to help. On my show, the police were typically portrayed as scoffers."

He chuckled. "If I was back on the force in St. Paul, I would probably be singing a different tune. But that's not the case in this small community. My staffing resources are limited, although I have access to area crime labs, and like I said, the state police and larger area police departments, when necessary. None of my officers are trained investigators, nor have any of them shown any interest in that area. The one who conducted some preliminary interviews on this case came back shaking her head, afraid she'd done more damage than gathered any helpful information. That's what brings me to you."

"Option of last resort," she said kiddingly.

He waved off her comment. "No, no, not at all. There's one more piece to this I've put off mentioning until you showed interest."

There was a catch. His offer was getting more and more intriguing. "Oh?"

"No cause for alarm. In fact, I think you'll appreciate the extra assistance."

Extra assistance? "And that would be?"

"You're not the only eyes and ears I have in that building, although you've got the distinction of being new with a unique background. An old crony from my days on the St. Paul force happens to be one of your neighbors. His name is Rex Alcorn."

"Rex?"

"Yes. Have you already met him?"

"He came to my aid the day I arrived and my sister wasn't home to greet me. Did he already agree to help you? And me?"

Goodhue ran a tongue over his lips, then smiled mysteriously. "Not exactly. Let's just say he's at our service in repayment of an old debt."

"I don't understand," she replied.

"No need for details at this time. If you say yes, he's ready to meet with you as soon as possible."

She wasn't quite ready to sign on just yet. She took a few sips of water while she delayed. After what she thought was the appropriate amount of time to pause, she framed her response. "I'll be happy to help you find the killer as long as we can agree on one thing."

"Right. We haven't talked compensation yet, have we?"

"Whatever you think is fair. No, what I need from you is your assurance that I can bow out at any time I feel this arrangement isn't working. The same would go for you, of course."

He narrowed his eyes. "Already talking about an escape clause? Should I be concerned?"

"Not particularly," she rushed to say. "It's just that I've never done this kind of thing before. For real anyhow. I don't want to build up your hopes. But I'll give it my best shot."

"That's all I ask," he said. "Do we have a deal?"

She hesitated just a beat. This was crazy, but if Scottie and Patty and now the chief thought she could do this, why not give it try? "Deal."

They shook on it.

"I'll email you all my case notes and will check in with you soon," Goodhue said. "And now, ladies, I'll leave you to finish your meal. On me. And Ms. Dane, Marla, if you could get with Rex as soon as you're done here, I'd appreciate it."

Her husband was barely out of the room before Patty spoke. "Thank you. I can tell you think my husband's proposal is beyond belief, but he's a smart guy. He doesn't do things he doesn't think will work."

"What do you think?" she couldn't help but ask.

"Me? I'm just an innocent bystander here," Patty replied, picking at the green salad she'd ordered.

Marla studied her while she waited for Patty to say more. When the other woman continued to pick at her lettuce and tomatoes, Marla laid it on the line. "Perhaps a bystander during the last few minutes. But innocent? No. I can't help thinking this extraordinary idea originated in your brain instead of your husband's."

Patty attempted to glance away, but she couldn't avoid Marla's stare for long.

"Okay, okay. Guilty. Just between us, I'll deny saying anything if you ever tell Colman or anyone else, including Rex Alcorn. Colman has found himself in over his head. After all the years he tried to get assigned to a homicide case without success, suddenly when he's least prepared and not staffed to handle one, here it is. He rejected the idea of asking for your help initially until I remembered something he'd told me about his old pal Rex. I don't know the details, but Rex seems to owe Colman a favor. A big one. I suggested he combine that with bringing you on board."

"I thought it was something like that."

"How did you figure it out?" Patty asked.

"Body language. I observed how you were almost mouthing the words for him, but you let him have center stage."

Patty pushed a chili pepper to the side of her salad plate. "You're good, Marla Dane. And notice I called you by that name and not Letitia Carruthers."

"Nothing special about it at all. Just close observation."

"Which is one part of what Colman wants you to do. The other part is to ask the right questions in the first place. Rex will be on board to help you analyze the responses."

The woman should be in sales. Better yet, she should consider puppetry. She'd already demonstrated how well she pulled the strings.

<h1 style="text-align:center">seven</h1>

. . .

Marla didn't have time to plan her first meeting with Rex Alcorn after Patty dropped her off at the condo complex because he called her as she was walking into the building. "We need to meet as soon as possible," he said without preamble. "Come to my place. I'm in 502."

"I'll be there in five minutes," she replied tersely. She needed time to get her mind around this new assignment. Five minutes wouldn't be enough, but it was as long as she felt she could stall.

Fortunately, Kitty was still out. Marla wouldn't have to tell her about her dinner with the wife of the chief of police until later. Kitty wouldn't relax until she coaxed some kind of story from her. Bringing her up to speed about working for the police would be saved for another day.

She took a few minutes to wash her face and hands and sip a little water. After a quick glance in the hall mirror and a pat down of her hair, which had somehow survived the rainstorm the day she arrived, she took a deep breath and headed for the lair of Rex Alcorn.

She had no idea what to expect from this first meeting. She didn't know him well enough to predict his mood or behavior, although from the brief encounter she'd had with him three days earlier, she wasn't enthusiastic.

She only had a moment to take in his condo. The living room anyhow. The walls appeared to be a medium shade of gray under the numerous nature pictures hung throughout. A dark tweed sectional facing the TV took up most of the room.

"What've you got so far?" he said before she even sat down in a wine-colored easy chair.

Her hand automatically felt for the necklace beneath her top as she took in his attire. Tonight he wore a dove gray knit pullover and dark charcoal pants. The color combination set off his dark sapphire eyes and graying hair. *Stop it, Marla.* He'd asked a question. Time to focus.

She could bottom-line things just like him. "Drake Elliot was supposedly single. He dated, and I use the term advisedly, at least one female resident and probably more, maybe even my sister, who claims she rebuffed his advances."

Rex nodded his head throughout her report but didn't comment.

Marla continued. "He attempted to get the first woman to invest in some kind of event. No more information on that. His MO was to wine and dine her over several dates that turned into overnights at local motels. When she refused to invest, he dumped her at the restaurant, leaving her to pay the bill."

She stopped.

"That it?" he asked.

"I just started this morning with time out for dinner, where I was propositioned by the local police chief to become one of his spies in the building."

"I couldn't find any criminal records on him. Not that he's never been arrested, but I suspect the name Drake Elliot is an alias."

"You have access to police files?" she asked, impressed even though she didn't want to be.

"Limited, now that I'm no longer active. So we already have a suspect?"

She held up a hand. "Wait! She claims she's innocent. She came to me before Chief Goodhue asked for my help. I started out doing this to help her prove she's not guilty by hopefully finding the real killer. I'm not so sure I'm ready to share any more that I know about her with you at this point."

He sat back, his two long arms straddling the arms of his own easy chair. "Then what good are you to this case?"

"I beg your pardon? I don't recall the term 'snitch' being used when I was asked to help the Maple Knolls police with this case."

He cocked his head. "Neither of us gets to pick and choose who is guilty of this murder. That's Rule Number One. No, actually Rule Number One is that only one of us can be in charge, and that's me."

She came out of her seat. "According to who? You? Not Chief Goodhue. At least he didn't mention anything like that when he asked for my help."

"Surely you don't think your creds as a fake PI qualify you to be in charge?"

"I never said that. But I don't plan to report to you, either."

He slammed both hands against his seated thighs. "What do you suggest then?"

She had to think fast. She had no idea how this should work, other than she didn't want to take orders from the man. "That we approach this assignment as a team. Surely you're familiar with that term from your police days?"

"Of course, but how do you see it working? We take turns being in charge? You get even days and I get the uneven ones?"

"No. Forget that approach, and not just because in some

months there are more uneven days than even," she replied, feeling like a kid smarting off to a parent. "I suggest we lay out an investigation plan now, break it down into its major parts and each of us take responsibility for those different areas."

Rex scraped his hands up and down the chair arms. "You might as well know, I'm not keen on doing this. I haven't spoken to Goodhue in ages. It's not like we're bosom buddies. We never were back in the old days, either. But I owe him, and I only agreed to help track down the killer to get me out from under that obligation."

She was aware of Goodhue's hold over him but until now didn't know how much that bugged him. "So much for explaining why you signed on, but what about my suggestion regarding the division of work?" she asked.

"Fine," he said dismissively. "If it gets us moving."

"I didn't bring my laptop. Do you have one?"

"No. I do everything on my phone. Why?"

"I thought we could lay out our plan on a computer," she said.

"I'll put it in the Notes app on my phone. What do you want to include?"

She wrinkled up her forehead. "I, uh, thought that's why you were along for the ride?"

He scratched his head. "You're saying I can't be in charge but it's up to me to come up with a plan?"

She considered. It did sound a bit presumptuous on her part. "Not the whole thing. Just get us started. How did you find killers back in St. Paul?"

He didn't reply immediately. "Start at the beginning, I guess," he said finally.

"The beginning? You mean when the body was found?"

"No. The beginning means breaking down our action steps. Maybe not in order; we can fix that later."

"Okay. What's the first step?"

"Let's start with the overall goal, identifying who wanted him dead and who could've done it," he said.

"And we do that how?"

"By talking to people, starting with those in the building," he said.

"Do you think we might have to go beyond the building?"

"Depends on what we learn from people here or if no one in this building fits the bill."

"I've already spoken to Tom Casey and got his take from whatever his coffee group said about Elliot."

"Good."

"And I'm planning to attend a wine and cheese party tomorrow night put on by the singles' social group."

"Even better. They ask me every time they get together. Seems they're perpetually short of single men. I turn them down most of the time. Will it look suspicious if I go also?"

"I don't know," she replied. "Will it? What kind of reputation do you have in the building?"

He crossed his arms in front of his chest. "You'll have to ask the others about that. I try to stay blissfully unaware of everyone else."

She couldn't help but laugh. "Good one, Alcorn. From what little I've been told, you seem to know everything that happens in this building. A plus for Goodhue besides your law enforcement training."

Now he laughed. "You give me too much credit, but I'll take it."

"Back to this plan. How do we talk to people? So far, my wits have gotten me by, but I need more to back me up. The next item needs to be coming up with questions."

"I suppose you think that's my job," he said.

"That's one task I think we can both handle," she replied.

"I'll try to recall some of the questions my alter ego, Letitia Carruthers, would ask."

"Okay, as long as whatever we ask gets us closer to the truth. To do that, we must analyze and filter everything we learn. That's another step."

"You should probably add information-gathering. We've already done some of that, but we'll need to keep researching to verify what we learn along the way."

Their dialogue continued for several more minutes. "This is a pretty good plan," Marla said at length, having gotten up to read over his shoulder.

"As much as it pains me to say it, we'll have to continue to check in with each other frequently," Rex said.

"Don't sound so aggrieved, Alcorn. We're gonna make a great team, as long as we treat each other as equals."

He rolled his eyes but didn't object. "Let's meet tomorrow morning and go over things again."

By the time they met at ten the next morning, she'd received the case notes from Goodhue. The case notes included a more specific description of the cause of death, including the fact that the victim had been drugged. The medical examiner estimated time of death between two and four in the morning. The package also held printouts of his Social Security and tax information, his credit card charges, telephone log, texts and emails. The first officer on the scene and investigating officer reports were also there, including Scottie's responses when questioned, word for word. No need to continue to hide the fact that Scottie was a suspect or at least a person of interest. Rex had probably known her identity the night before and just put Marla through the wringer to see what she'd do.

Devouring the sum of Elliot's life, what little the police had been able to find on the man, kept her reading until midnight.

Hopefully this morning she could stay awake as she and Rex planned their day.

"What did you pick up from Goodhue's case notes?" Rex asked before she had a chance to sit down.

"Good morning to you, too, partner," she replied, seating herself on one end of the sectional without invitation. "My main takeaway is that we know more about him dead than we do alive."

"Yeah, that was my impression as well. Not a good start. We have a lot more to discover about the man. Where do you suggest we start?"

"We reinterview Scottie Richards. You should've told me last night you already knew she was the person the police had questioned instead of letting me refuse to give up her name. Not the best start of our partnership."

Her comment didn't appear to throw him. "I wanted to see how loyal you'd be to her," he replied. "Loyalty can work against you sometimes when you let it count more than the truth."

He had a point, but she still didn't like having been put on the spot the night before. "I'll keep that in mind," she said.

"Why interview her again?"

"Why?"

"Humor me."

The reasons for talking to Scottie again seemed obvious, but fine, she could play this game. "First, by now, her tears should've dried so we can get a clearer story from her. Since she's the one who set me looking into the murder in motion, she'll want to be of assistance. That may not be the case with anyone else we interview, so let's take advantage of her willingness to help. And finally, having thought more about it, hopefully she'll have other names to suggest."

He was staring at her when she finished.

"What?" she asked.

"Your logic is right on point."

"That's a surprise?" she asked. Why did even a compliment from this man sound more like a putdown?

"A relief. You aren't a total novice. Your ability to think logically as well as what you may have picked up on that TV show and stored away in the back of your brain may just work to our advantage after all."

"Good to know. I can relax now. I was afraid I wouldn't be able to measure up to your standards."

His blues bored into her. "You're being facetious. I was sincere."

Had their relationship turned a corner and she'd missed it? "Sorry. If you were sincere, then thank you."

Her phone rang before Rex could respond. "Ms. Dane? Marla?" Chief Goodhue asked.

"Yes, Chief? What's up?"

"That's what I'm calling to ask you. Did you and Alcorn get together to compare notes yet?"

"As we speak," she replied. It hadn't even been twenty-four hours, barely twelve, since he'd asked her to get involved with his case. The long arm of the law apparently was shorter than she'd imagined. "In fact, this is the second time we've talked."

"And? Where do we stand?" Goodhue asked.

Marla raised a brow as she glanced at Rex. "We're just about to start our interviews."

"Good, good. Keep me posted."

"What did he want?" Rex asked when she hung up.

"An update? How fast does he expect us to find this killer?"

"Already. He's a man of high expectations."

"I guess," she replied.

"While we're on the subject of interviewing folks, let's go over some pointers," Rex said. "If you don't mind the advice, that is?"

"Okay."

"The trick is to let whoever you're interviewing do most of the talking," he said. "That's not always easy, because some have learned the less they say, the better. And that can include the innocent ones; they're just smart enough to keep their mouths shut."

"I'll keep that in mind."

"But if they do start to talk, let them. See where it takes you. And use follow-up questions."

She gave him a mock salute.

"You probably should've added, 'Aye, aye, sir,'" he said kiddingly.

"An oversight. I still can, if you'd prefer."

She returned to the sectional, where he joined her a respectable foot away. "I'm glad my persona hasn't scared you away. You even joke with me."

"The alternative would be constant conflict and misunderstanding. Neither of us wants that, do we? You have your reasons for signing on, and I have mine."

He tilted his head slightly. For the first time, she saw the gold circles around the darker irises. "You know mine, but you haven't said why you joined this rodeo."

"I thought I told you. One of his almost-victims, Scottie Richards, is afraid she'll be charged with the murder despite her claims of innocence. I only agreed to help after she pushed." No need to tell him about Scottie's promise to call her friend in LA.

"But you're new here. You probably just met her."

"Good read. The truth is, I arrived in town at loose ends. You already know a little about what happened in LA. What the headlines would have you believe. But much more went down. I don't want to go into it, but suffice it to say, I needed to get away. But I'm not dabbling with this case because I was bored. I know this is serious business, and I'm prepared to give it my all."

He studied her a moment too long, then changed focus.

"Then we're good for tonight. I don't think we can prepare further. I don't plan to stick around the shindig very long, but don't let my early departure change your plans. Meet me here at ten and we can share intel."

They seemed to be meeting a lot in his condo. With other guys she might be somewhat concerned. But she could trust Rex Alcorn. Couldn't she?

eight

* * *

"You're going to wear that tonight?" Kitty asked as she and Marla dressed for the wine and cheese party.

Marla studied her choice of designer blue jeans and white pullover. She'd discarded the idea of wearing a pantsuit or dress in favor of a more casual outfit. Understated, elegant casual, but casual just the same. "What's wrong with these? We're not going to the opera or some other fancy bash. Isn't this just a group of neighbors getting together to drink wine and check each other out?"

"Well, yes, but it'll be your first time to meet most of these folks. You're a famous TV star. Don't you want to impress them?"

"I'm not here to impress people with my celebrity. In fact, I'm trying to downplay it."

"Not by playing *investigator* again," Kitty replied.

"The one thing I learned by playing Letitia was that good investigators are supposed to be part of the background and not draw attention to themselves."

Kitty narrowed her eyes. "That's why you were always in some bright-colored pantsuit?"

"I said 'supposed to be.' The wardrobe mistress didn't get the message. As much as I liked the ensembles she dressed me in, my days of pantsuits, designer dresses and eight-hundred-dollar shoes are over. All I want to wear these days are blue jeans, cover-ups and ballet flats. Much more comfortable."

"But you did bring a few of those items with you. I already checked your closet."

Marla could only laugh. "Of course you did, little sister. Some things never change."

"Too bad I'm two inches shorter than you or I'd be begging to wear one tonight." She pouted like she had when they were teens and Marla wouldn't let her wear her new blouse. "But before you launch into your new wardrobe, have another think about a pantsuit. Maybe Letitia attempted to blend into the woodwork, technicolor presence notwithstanding, but if you want the gang here to take you seriously as an investigator, reinforce their memories of Letitia."

"But ..." She didn't finish the thought. "I hate to admit it, but you're right. I came here wanting to escape my old life. And I no sooner started getting used to the more casual me than I signed on to this murder investigation." Then she remembered that Kitty didn't know about her deal with the Maple Knolls police department. "Scratch that. 'Signed on' sounds too formal for what I agreed to do for Scottie.."

In the end, Marla wore the emerald green pantsuit she'd been allowed to take from the show after the third season. Kitty might not be crazy about this undercover investigation, but she knew her fellow residents better than Marla. Still, to tone it down, Marla selected an ecru tee to go under it.

Fortunately, with her mind focused on the evening's event as well as playing wardrobe consultant to Marla, Kitty didn't ask about Marla's dinner with Patty Goodhue the night before. But Marla didn't kid herself. The subject would come up sooner rather than later. She'd better be ready with an explanation.

Kitty accompanied her to the party to introduce her to the hostess, Shipton. "You'll like Naomi," she said as they made their way to Naomi's condo. "She and her neighbor across the hall, Billy Warren, have been a bit of a thing for a while now, although they're not interested in marriage. They seem to like their independence. They're social people and take turns hosting get-togethers, even for those who aren't singles."

"Good to know. I'll make sure to chat them up at some point. Find out what rumors they've heard."

"You can ignore the guys. Most of them show up for the free food and drink, which is a continued irritant of the single women who'll be there. These guys are not looking for a mate. Maybe a roll in the hay, some not even that. They're pretty set in their single lives."

"Anyone I should avoid?" Marla asked.

"Besides me, no. Make the rounds."

Marla pulled up. Was that some kind of veiled threat or just Kitty trying to be funny? "Why should I avoid you?"

Kitty played with an earring. "I could say I was kidding, but I'd be lying. As much as I wanted you to get involved here at Rambling Meadows, I never pictured you participating in a murder investigation. You haven't told me a lot about the aftermath of being let go from that show, but I can't help sensing there's so much more you're not telling me. You don't have to let me in until you're ready, if ever. But it seems to me like you're using this investigation to put off dealing with whatever you're running away from."

Marla started to rebut Kitty's supposition but stopped. Was she right?

Kitty seemed to sense her sister's confusion. "Look, you asked and I told you. Crappy timing, but that's me. At least it was honest. Table it for now. You've got more than enough on your plate tonight. I'll be there as your wing woman."

True to her word, Kitty did exactly that when they arrived at Naomi's condo. When she introduced Marla to the hostess, she made sure they each knew enough about the other to engage in light conversation.

"I'm so glad you could join us tonight," Naomi told Marla. "I'm honored to have someone with your background as my guest."

"I'm flattered," Marla replied, resorting to her standard reply from her LA days. "I'm so glad you decided to still have the party in light of recent events."

"Ah, you're referring to what happened to that poor Drake Elliot."

"Yes. My first week here and there's a murder."

"You should be used to that, what with solving one every week on TV," Naomi said.

Yet another person to set straight. Marla debated how far to go with this topic. "That was different. I'm not Letitia Carruthers. I'm an actress. I only solved those make-believe murders because someone else provided me with the words and action." She looked her hostess in the eye. "It's just unnerving when the very thing I spent the last six years pretending to do has now shown up almost on my doorstep." Well, her front yard.

Naomi arched a brow. "Unnerving? Is it because they haven't found the murderer yet?"

"Well, yes."

"Don't let it get to you. We live in a secure building. No one's going to get in here unless they're let in."

Did she really believe her own words?

Marla leaned in close to the woman and lowered her voice as she spoke. "What if someone who lives in the building or has ready access to it is the killer?"

"Surely you don't believe that?" her hostess said.

"Chalk it up to my being the newcomer, I guess. I'm still getting my bearings here."

"That's understandable. Tell you what. Relax tonight. Get to know your neighbors. Let's get you fixed up with a drink, then I'll introduce you to a few folks."

She couldn't have asked for a better setup. She let Naomi take the lead.

"Damien Chutney, I'd like you to meet Kitty Lovejoy's sister, Marla Dane. Marla, this gentleman has lived in the complex longer than the rest of us. He moved in the week it opened."

"A longtime resident," Marla said, shaking his hand. "I'll bet you've seen your share of changes to the building since you've been here."

"Ain't you that movie star they've all been gossiping about?" Chutney said in response.

She couldn't tell if his question was curious or accusatory. "I've done a few movies but not recently," she replied. "I have been on television, though."

"Right. Got it mixed up. You were some kind of policewoman."

"Private investigator."

"Why are you here then? Have they moved your show to Minnesota?"

She had to laugh. This was a new one. Points to Chutney for originality. "No, although that would've been an interesting switch. Instead, the powers that be decided to make my character younger. While I'm negotiating new projects, I'm visiting my sister."

"Kitty, yes. We've had our run-ins since she moved in, but she's a pretty good egg for the most part."

"She'll be glad to know that," Marla replied, debating how

she could guide him to the topic of the murder. "Since you're such a longtime resident, you must like it here."

"Like it? More like it's too expensive to go elsewhere," he grumbled.

"I guess condo prices have increased considerably since you purchased your place. But you're here tonight and not holed up in your own place, so that tells me you do socialize with the other residents."

He snorted. "Don't peg me as some sort of social butterfly, Ms., uh ..."

"Dane," she replied, keeping her smile plastered in place.

"I'm here because Naomi is my sister and she promised there'd be food. Especially hors d'oeuvres. Otherwise, I pretty much stick to myself."

"That's a shame. I hoped you could clue me in about the others here tonight," she said.

"Why're you asking? Looking for a man?"

"No, why would you think that?"

"It's a singles party. Why else would you come?" he asked.

She offered a confidential look. "I had to get out of the condo. Kitty has been driving me nuts."

He chuckled. "Now that makes more sense. She usually gravitates to the younger guys when she deigns to join us. I'm not exactly her type." He paused long enough to glance about the room. "Who'd ya want to know about? Surely not the richest guys here? I suspect your bank account far exceeds theirs."

If he only knew the precarious state of her finances. "The media make it sound like television stars amass huge fortunes, but they also have an army of support staff to pay. Anyway, since a murder took place here, I want to be reassured my sister is safe."

"The guy got killed on the grounds, NOT inside the building. Big difference."

"Surely you don't think someone off the street just walked up to the man and offed him?" she asked, having found her way to her preferred subject.

"Why not? This building's as secure as Fort Knox. Well, maybe not that safe, but you get the picture. Besides, he was my neighbor, and I never saw anyone suspicious going into or coming out of his condo."

Well, duh! Why hadn't it occurred to her to identify Elliot's neighbors? Only dumb luck now that Damien Chutney brought up the idea. "He was your neighbor, huh? How well did you know him?"

"Didn't. Who'da thunk since I'm such an agreeable guy. But he coulda cared less about me once he learned my bank account suffered after my divorce fifteen years back."

Interesting. "What happened?" she asked. "Did he want to borrow money from you?"

"Nothing like that. We walked into the building together one day shortly after he took up residence next to my condo. My daughter, who lives in Mendota Heights, asked me to keep some of the Christmas gifts she'd purchased for her husband. I looked like I'd struck it rich with the fancy suit bag and shoe box I had in tow. He raised a brow and said as much, but I set him straight right away."

"No more mention of money after that?" she asked.

Damien Chutney gave her question some thought. "Now that you ask, yeah, once more a month or so later. We were in the elevator with one of the women who's here tonight. Rhonda, no, Rita Haley, the one with the mousy brown hair who's helping out in the kitchen. She got off before we did, and once we were alone, he turned to me and asked if that was a real diamond bracelet she was wearing. How was I supposed to know? Which is how I replied. Then he asked if I knew who she was and I told him.

"But he wasn't done with his questions. He wanted to know what her marital situation was. Said he hadn't seen a wedding ring on her left hand, but you couldn't go by that so much anymore. I replied that I'd heard she'd gotten divorced a few months before and was now living here alone."

"His questions didn't seem strange or too nosy to you?" she asked.

He stared her down. "Lady, Marla, when you live in a building like this, just about everyone wants to know everyone else's business."

"I get the idea."

She was running out of questions, and Damien Chutney appeared to be tiring of their conversation. "Please excuse me. I see my sister over there motioning me. It was nice to meet you."

"Yeah, right," he called to her escaping back.

She'd learned a little more about Drake Elliot from talking to Damien Chutney, but it had been a strain. Hopefully her next attempt at interrogation would be more successful.

nine

· · ·

Marla hit the refreshment table while she figured out who to approach next.

"I hear you're Kitty's sister," a male voice said, right behind her.

She swiveled tentatively toward the voice, attempting to avoid collision with the body attached to it. "That's right. I'm Marla Dane." He was too close to offer her his hand. "And you would be?"

"Pete Gordon. I've been reading all about you. Is it true you decked the 'new girl,' Julia Wainwright?"

"Who have you been reading? That's a new one on me," she replied, tamping down her anger. Someone was still busy manufacturing untruths about her. Probably Julia's PR person.

He shrugged. "Couldn't tell you. I just picked up one of those gossip rags while waiting in line at the grocery store. Apparently the story's not true?"

Despite not wanting to get into anything about the show, if she fed him something, he might be more amenable to sharing what he knew about Elliot. "In one of my earlier shows in which Julia guest-starred, she was a suspect I was following, and the script called for me to launch myself at her to keep her from running away. The scene was well-choreographed, but Julia missed her cue and wound up falling harder than she should have. In all fairness to her, a high-powered visitor on the set forgot to turn off her phone, and it went off just as Julia was supposed to block her fall."

That wasn't exactly the case. Julia had been hung over that morning and really had missed her cue, but why put her down now?

Gordon rubbed his neck. "Too bad. Thought I'd stumbled across a hot story I could tell folks around here. Everyone's curious about you."

"Really? I thought Kitty would've filled everyone in by now."

He poured her a glass of white wine after she indicated which she wanted. "Kitty just hits the high points."

Her curiosity got the better of her. "And those would be?" she asked.

"How one of those rags I mentioned put you in the top ten women over fifty on television, your fancy-schmancy home in Westwood, all the great wardrobe you got to keep ..." He broke off long enough to take in what she was wearing. "Surely those duds didn't come from your show?"

Nice guy. How soon could she get away from this one?

"I not only wore this pantsuit on the show, it's an Alexander McQueen. It was chosen specifically to go with my red hair. Kitty suggested I wear it."

At the mention of the famous designer, his scowl changed to a smile. "Guess it's not that bad. Looks good on you."

"Thanks. Now that I've passed muster, let's get down to business."

He raised a bushy eyebrow. "And that would be?"

"Helping me get to know the others here in the building."

"Why does that matter?" he asked.

"I plan to be here a while. That being the case, I want to know my neighbors."

"Thought you were 'just between projects'?"

"I am, but there's no telling how long before my plans come together. I needed to get away from the environment in LA. Catch my breath back here on Minnesota soil."

"Let's go over there to that love seat and talk," he said, emphasizing the word *love* and taking her elbow. "I'd prefer my neighbors not hear me talking with you."

"Oh?" she said as she took her seat, keeping as much distance between them as possible. "Have you got some hot gossip to share?"

"Gossip, no. I heard through the condo grapevine that you're interested in knowing more about Drake Elliot and his murder even though you supposedly came here to get away from that sort of thing."

Where had he picked up on that? It was true, but she'd spoken only with Scottie, Kitty and Tom Casey thus far, and they were sworn to secrecy. "I just wasn't expecting to come back home to a murder."

"Not so easy for the rest of us to believe, either."

"You at least know your neighbors. I don't know anyone except my sister."

A knowing look settled on his face. "You wanna know about your neighbors, I could fill you in, but the price is dinner. My treat."

She should've known he'd attempt to finesse her simple statement about not knowing her neighbors into a date. How much did she want to know whatever he had to reveal? And did he really have anything to tell in the first place?

"Dinner? I don't think so," she replied.

"Lunch then?"

 Barbara Barrett

He wasn't ready to drop this. "Coffee," she replied, knowing full well he had his coffee klatch every morning.

"Okay. Coffee Saturday morning," he replied. "That's just two days away."

Foiled! Tom Casey had told her the coffee group only met on weekday mornings. Peters had outsmarted her. The most she could hope was that she and Rex would get the info they needed in the interim so she could break her date. "Okay."

The date made, she fished for a reason to move on. Once again, she used the refreshment table as her excuse.

"Try my new cream cheese dip," Naomi said, coming up to her. "Billy found the recipe in some magazine and insisted I try it."

Although she didn't typically indulge in dips and chips, she put a hefty dollop of the concoction on a few corn chips. When Naomi continued to watch her, she had no recourse but to take a few bites.

It didn't taste terrible. Cream cheese just wasn't one of her favorites. She let her tongue roam over the residue that remained in her mouth. An unfamiliar flavor clobbered her senses.

"What's in this recipe, Naomi?" she asked as politely as she could despite her growing suspicion about the ingredients.

"Let me think," her hostess replied, attempting to remember. "Cream cheese, obviously. And a touch of garlic powder, lemon juice, and, oh, chopped hazelnut."

Hazelnut! Her nemesis. One of them, anyhow. She had to get out of there. "I just remembered a call that's coming in from LA tonight. Thank you for inviting me, but I have to go." That was about as much civility as she could muster. Time to fly.

What an end to her investigative efforts.

Her brain was on overdrive. Had she even thought to bring her antihistamine with her from LA? She hadn't experienced an allergic reaction in years, once her allergist figured out she had a food allergy to hazelnuts.

She could already feel the rash breaking out on her palms. Rex's condo was just down the hall. She'd seen him leave the party at least ten minutes prior. She headed that direction.

"You're early," he said to her back as she rushed past him into the room.

"I need your help! I ate the wrong thing and now I'm breaking out." She showed him her palms. They were red, just starting to show signs of the telltale bumps.

He examined her hands. "Doesn't look good. What is it?"

She attempted to tell him what happened before it became too difficult to speak. "Hazel. Nuts. In dip. Allergic. Need anti-histamine."

"What do we do?"

"Need EpiPen."

"And I take it you don't have one. Let's go," he said, steering her toward the door.

"Go?"

"There's an urgent care three blocks away. I'm driving you there. Try to hang on until we get there."

Easier said than done. From past experience, she knew not to scratch. That only spread the rash faster. But not doing so cost her whatever comfort she still possessed.

Rex had to help her out of the car and explain her condition to the receptionist. Though she wasn't used to such assistance, she had no choice but to let him take the lead. When the young guy at the desk didn't respond quickly enough, Rex summoned the physician on duty. "Can't you folks see she's getting worse by the minute?" he said in a tone that must have been used frequently in his law enforcement days to secure order. "Give her something to get her breathing right again."

His directive bore immediate results. While they monitored her blood pressure, she was given oxygen and then epinephrine.

Rex didn't leave her side.

"How're you doing?" he asked several minutes after she'd been treated.

"Much better, thanks to your quick actions."

"Every so often those annual first aid refresher courses I was required to take come in handy. They want to observe you another hour to ensure your blood pressure is coming down."

"I know the drill. I'm sorry you got pulled into this, but I'm glad you were there," she told him sincerely.

He studied her for several beats. "This happens often?"

"Until my doctors figured out what was triggering the reaction. At first, they thought it was the pressure of appearing on a weekly television show, but they quickly ruled that out. For the first two years, I had an EpiPen with me at all times, but when I seemed to have my allergies under control, I switched to my ever-present antihistamine tablets."

Rex fished in her purse for her phone when it rang. "It's Goodhue. Okay if I answer for you?"

She nodded. Rex put her on speaker so she could hear the other end of the call.

"No, we don't know who the killer is yet," Rex told their caller.

"You're still working at this time of day?" Goodhue said.

"Marla had a bit of an incident," Rex said. "An allergic reaction to something she ate a singles party at Rambling Meadows we attended to gain some intel."

"Is she okay?" Concern underlay the chief's tone.

"Now. She didn't have an EpiPen with her, so I brought her to an urgent care. We're waiting for the doc to release her so she can go home and get some needed rest."

"Good grief. Is she okay otherwise?"

"I'm fine, Chief. Like Rex, we're just waiting for my blood pressure to stabilize. I'll be fine tomorrow. In fact, we've been planning tomorrow's agenda. We want to search Elliot's condo, but we'll need you to intercede with the building manager."

"Sure. First thing in the morning I'll call her. We'll talk more then. You get some rest."

"I thought we wouldn't hear from him until at least tomorrow morning," she said once Rex put her phone away.

"The mayor must be pressuring him for results," Rex said. "Since we have to stick around here a little longer, do you feel up to discussing whatever you learned at the party?"

"Sure. I hope I didn't forget anything amid all this excitement." She recounted what Damien Chutney had told her about Elliot. "Which brings up another item to add to our to-do list. We need to know who lives where in this building, particularly near Elliot's digs."

"Got that covered."

She chuckled, as much as she could given her condition. "I should've known. We should've started there."

"The police investigator took care of that, although his notes were pretty sparse. The older lady who lived across the hall characterized Elliot as a 'nice boy' who 'didn't make any noise.' Kaitlin Fargo, who lived next door to him, said she hardly knew him. And your boy Damien Chutney, who lived on the other side, asked him over for drinks, but Elliot was on his way out of the building."

"Either they preferred not to share any information with the police or they really didn't know much about him," she said. "If the latter was the case, then Elliot kept a low profile in the building."

"That part fits what little we do know," he replied. "Probably didn't want to bring any undue attention to himself while he set up his marks."

"Thanks to Damien Chutney, we know Rita Haley might have been one of them."

"How do you suggest we get her to come clean about having had anything to do with him?"

"The direct way."

"And if that doesn't work?" he asked.

"The direct way, part two."

"Not very creative."

She held up the arm with the blood pressure cuff on it. "Why do you think that is?"

"We can hold off until tomorrow if you want," he said.

"I'd prefer to stay at it for now." Actually, she'd prefer to be back in her bed at Kitty's sound asleep, but that was out of the question at the moment.

"Hold up. I'll be right back," he said. He returned shortly and held out a paper cup to her. "They said you could have water. Nothing stronger yet."

She took the water and surprised herself with how thirsty she was. "Thanks. This another step in your first aid training?"

"No. Just something I thought you might want. Whenever things start to stall out for me, I turn to the stuff. Hydrate."

"I only had enough time to glance at the notes Goodhue sent us. How about you? Have you had longer to review his finances, his credit card charges in particular?"

"Yeah. Why do you ask?" he said.

"For starters, what did they tell you?" she asked.

"Whatever funds he was taking in for his investment schemes weren't making their way into his bank accounts. He had two, one apparently for day-to-day operational expenses, the other for larger items. Whatever he took in from his scams is somewhere else. They didn't find it when they went through his condo, but they probably didn't know about his background at that time and didn't do a deep search."

"Which we'll do tomorrow when we search his condo," she said.

"Yeah, but I'm betting he stuck it away elsewhere. Maybe even divided it up so if someone forced him to give it over, they wouldn't get it all."

"What about the credit card charges?" she asked.

"He lived on his credit card, if that's what you wanted to know."

"Did you analyze them further?"

"Split them into type of expense: food, utilities, rent, lodging, that kind of thing."

"He didn't own the condo?"

"Apparently not. The rental payments were going to a rent manager. Didn't have time to get the name of the owner, but we can do that tomorrow too."

"Good. I don't know if it's necessary, but you never know," she replied. "Did you study the dates of his restaurant and lodging charges?"

"Just the basics, mainly the locations. He seemed to have three preferred restaurants and a larger list of motels. Where are you going with this?"

"I want to see if there's a pattern. I'm not sure if it will tell us if he worked each mark one at a time or if he combined them, but if it's the former, then maybe we can get an idea how many there were since he moved into the building."

"Do you suppose they'd give me some of that epinephrine?" he asked. "It seems to be doing wonders for your brain."

ten

. . .

The urgent care doc was willing to dismiss Marla to return home provided someone stayed with her. "No problem, my sister's there," she told him.

However, Kitty wasn't there when she walked in the door of the condo. Then and only then did Marla check her phone messages.

"Got to talking to Bruce Cranston at the party. Found we both like noir movies. Going to his place to check out one I haven't seen. Don't wait up for me."

Rex heard. "So that's Bruce's new line. Film noir. Never would've suspected Kitty of being into those."

"Me either, but you know my sister."

An awkward silence filled the room. Finally, Marla attempted to end it. "She didn't say she wouldn't be home at all. I'll be fine until she gets here."

"And if you're not? If you wake up with a reaction to the meds they gave you or the rash comes back, what'll you do then?"

"Call you?" she offered in a timid voice.

"I'll just stay here."

"Where? I'm in the guest room."

"The couch in the living room then. I can sleep anywhere."

Thank you, Kitty. Once again you've made me beholden to Rex Alcorn. He's the last person I want staying overnight. "I'll find you some bedding."

"You want to go right to sleep?" he asked.

"I thought you did."

"I'll be fine out here in the living room, if you're tired. After the last few hours, you probably should get some rest."

"I should, I know. But I'm wide awake. Do you want to discuss the case some more?"

"Got any beer?"

"We'll have to check. I don't drink the stuff, but I'm guessing Kitty keeps it for visitors."

A quick search of the fridge resulted in a major brand of brewski for him, and she pulled out one of her Diet Cokes. A minute later, they were seated on the same couch where he was supposed to sleep. Rather than following up on the case, she asked him another question instead. "Why are you here, Rex? Here meaning living in this building."

"No one's ever asked me that before. Not even the building manager when I moved in."

Had she inadvertently touched a nerve? It had occurred to her out of the blue, and she blurted it out. "You don't have to answer."

"I will. I'm just considering what to say," he said.

"Is it that difficult?"

He placed his hands on his knees and leaned in. "I took a disability retirement from the force ten years ago. My marriage had already broken up a few years before. Police officers don't have great track records with their marriages. That trend held true for me. We sold the house as part of our divorce settlement. I stuck my share in the bank and rented a cheap apartment the next few years. When I found myself retiring early, I wanted to upgrade. My daughter suggested this place. She thought I needed to be somewhere classy around people. I never would've seen myself here otherwise, but once I did the tour, I decided this would be my new life."

His lengthy explanation surprised her. Thus far, Rex had been a man of a few words. And very private. What she'd just heard came from a different person. "What prompted you to take a disability retirement?"

"I made a dumb move and tackled a perp the wrong way. Broke my right leg and injured my ACL."

"Does it still give you trouble?" she couldn't help asking.

"On occasion. I walk every day or get on the treadmill in winter, but that's the extent of my exercise."

"Was your injury related to whatever it is you owe Colman Goodhue?"

His whole body tensed. She not only saw but she felt him freeze up.

"Are you ready to tell me what really brought you back to Minnesota?" he asked instead of answering her question.

She backed away an inch, although it felt more like a mile. "I did tell you."

"I'm pretty sure that was just your cover story."

She didn't reply at first. She'd underestimated Rex and his ability to read behind the headlines. "Touché, Alcorn. You found a way to keep me from pressing you further on that topic."

"Maybe someday I'll share a little about my relationship with Goodhue, but we don't know each other well enough yet."

"I don't know if I'll ever be able or want to talk about my real reason for being here. From what you've shown me thus far about your far-reaching connections, I wouldn't be surprised if you unearthed my story out in LA. But I hope you won't."

"As long as you're not on the lam, I'll leave that part of your life alone. You're not, are you?" he teased.

Rex Alcorn was making a joke? She couldn't resist playing along. She placed a finger over her mouth. "I should've known your being an ex-cop and all you'd be onto me. I ran a traffic light in Arizona and didn't pay my bill at the motel where I stayed in Missouri before I got here."

He didn't even blink. "Quite a feat to pull off when I for one know you flew here from California."

This guy wouldn't let her get away with anything. That made her feel good.

"Enough about my life of crime. Let's talk about you. You have a daughter? Tell me about her."

"Ah, Cathie. The one good thing that came out of my marriage. She's in her late thirties, married, mother of two boys under ten, and she's a psychologist over in Eden Prairie."

"And her husband?"

"Teaches American History at the University of Minnesota."

"I wouldn't have pictured you as a grandfather."

"No? Why not?" he asked.

"Just ... I don't know. I can't imagine little kids calling you Grandpa."

"They don't. I'm Gramps."

They sat in silence a bit before he spoke again. "How 'bout you? Any children?"

"None of my own. I thought myself too old when I married Hugo. But I am stepmom to his children. Selena is 35, and Joshua is 32. We aren't close because their mother kept them away from him as much as she was legally able."

"Too bad."

"Being separated from them hurt him more than he would admit. At least they were there for him at the end."

"No grandkids?"

"Not that I know of. They're both single, although that doesn't mean anything."

"And it's just you and Kitty? No other siblings?" he asked.

"No. It's just the two of us. Why did you ask about that?"

"If I give it to you straight, you probably won't like what you hear."

"Lay it on me."

He took a breath before proceeding. "I think coming here to Kitty's was your option of last resort. Your sister clearly loves you, but she can't see how much you're hurting because she's so wrapped up in her own life."

"That's not true!" She and Kitty had always been different from each other, but that didn't weaken their sisterly bond. "Kitty has been on me for months to leave LA and come live with her."

"I'm not disputing her motivation. She's just trying to help you but in her way. The only way she knows. My guess is she's unaware of what all you've been through in the last few months. She couldn't be because the environment you've been living in all these years is totally foreign to her."

She attempted to rebut his theory but couldn't find the words. He'd called it correctly.

"I warned you," he said when she didn't reply.

"Don't condemn Kitty. She's had more than enough to deal with the last few years with an unfaithful husband and difficult divorce."

He took the time to consider her response. "Okay. You're more forgiving than I'd be, but she's your sister."

"She's not completely unaware of my situation. But you're right. I've never shared the realities of my life as a so-called celebrity with her. It's been easier to concentrate on the glitz and glamour. She understands that better."

He didn't reply for several beats.

"What aren't you saying?" she asked.

"I didn't realize you understood her so well. I'm impressed." He swiveled to eye her directly. "Even recuperating from an allergic reaction with all those meds running through your system, you're a decent person."

eleven

. . .

The aroma of fresh coffee woke her.

"It's about time you decided to join the rest of the world," Kitty said, entering the living room with a mug and setting it on the side table. "Too much wine last night to make it to your bed?" Her tone, though accusatory, mainly carried an undertone of humor.

Marla rubbed her eyes and took a few deep breaths before sitting up. What was she doing here on the living room sofa? The last she remembered, she and Rex were talking about families. His and hers. He'd made a comment about her relationship with Kitty, but all she recalled of it now was a weird feeling she'd revealed more to him than she planned. But the specifics escaped her.

What happened to Rex? Had he fallen asleep too? Had he still been here when Kitty arrived home? And just when had Kitty come in?

"You look absolutely zapped. Drink your coffee."

Marla ran a hand through her hair, still attempting to get her bearings. Then she took her sister's advice and sipped the brew.

Kitty made it too strong. Must be a Midwestern thing Marla had abandoned on the West Coast.

Kitty left her alone while she fussed about something in the kitchen. Within a minute, the smell of bacon caught up with Marla's nostrils. That was strange. Kitty never had more than cold cereal and skim milk for breakfast.

A few seconds later, Kitty bounced back into the room. "Would you mind clearing out to your room? I have company coming for breakfast."

Rather than ask who, Marla merely raised a brow.

"Bruce Cranston. You wouldn't have met him last night because the two of us left early to check out his films."

"I got your phone message when I got back here."

She watched Kitty hustling around attempting to put an already clean room in order. "Where is all this energy coming from, Kitty?"

Kitty stopped long enough to appear puzzled. "What do you mean?"

"I assume you spent the night with him, and now here you are, bustling around ready to entertain him at this time of morning. When did you sleep?"

"Oh, that," Kitty replied dismissively. "Funny thing. His films were boring beyond belief. I fell asleep on the couch in his media room. Apparently he followed suit about a half hour later." She made a face. "I hate getting older. I used to be able to stay up all night and go to class without missing a beat."

"That was forty years ago, sis."

"Is that why you crashed out here?"

Might as well bring her up to speed. "I inadvertently ate some dip that contained chopped-up hazelnuts. I broke out in a rash almost immediately. Rex took me to urgent care and then stayed with me until the meds they gave me worked their way through my system. I guess, like you, I fell asleep out here while we talked."

"Rex stayed the night?" Kitty's voice rose suggestively.

"Sorry, can't answer that. He obviously was gone by whenever you got in, but I was out for the night once I closed my eyes."

"Is something going on between you and Rex?"

Kitty still didn't know that Colman Goodhue had prevailed upon Marla to work with his police department and Rex. Marla wasn't ready to bring her sister on board with that arrangement yet. She had to leave Kitty hanging where Rex was concerned.

"The only thing going on with him is that he's come to my aid twice already since I've been here."

"Well, I'm sorry, Marla. As much as I want you here, I can't be here for you every minute."

"I don't expect that, Kitty. I just explained how it was that Rex has been around."

"Okay, okay," Kitty said, calming down. "I guess I'm just anxious about Bruce showing up any minute."

"Why is that? You have male guests here all the time, don't you?"

Kitty placed a hand on her chest, imitating a Southern belle. "Why Marla Dane, you must think me some kind of coquette. I'll admit to still having an active libido, but that door over there isn't a revolving model."

This discussion was quickly escalating into something Marla didn't want to get into. "Sorry, Kitty. I don't want to argue with you. It's too early in the morning. My brain's still not working properly, although thanks to the coffee, I'm slowly reviving."

Marla left things like that and wandered back to her room. It was quarter to seven. Still early for her. She took her half-finished cup of coffee with her and texted Rex.

> What happened? Did you leave after I fell asleep or …?

Let's talk. When can we meet?

> Give me another hour.

See you at 8.

She set her alarm for seven forty-five and headed to bed.

She made it to Rex's condo with two minutes to spare. Her hair was still a tad wet, but she was glad she spent more time sleeping than showering.

"Okay, what all went on last night?" she asked, settling comfortably into his easy chair.

He returned a lascivious smile. "Are you sure you want to know?"

"Can the lewd attitude, Alcorn. I'd know if I had something to really be worried about. I just want to know when I dropped off to sleep and how much longer you hung around."

"Worried about your snoring?" he joked. "Okay, you were out before midnight. I kept waiting for Kitty to return so I could leave. Then I conked out too. I woke up around three. Still no Kitty, but you were completely out, so I took off, locking the door behind me."

"Thanks for looking after me. Especially since Kitty appears to have been out most of the night. She claims she fell asleep on the couch in Bruce's media room. And now, if you can believe it, she's cooking him a full breakfast in her kitchen."

"And you didn't invite me?"

"No way! She was already speculating about the amount of time I've been spending with you."

"You clued her in about our partnership?"

"She knows what I've been trying to do, because she was

there when Scottie approached me, but not that Goodhue asked for my help or that he teamed me up with you," she told him.

"Wait a minute. Does that mean she thinks you and I are, uh, a thing?"

She couldn't identify his tone. Incredulity? Amusement? Or perhaps delight? "Nah, I talked her out of that idea by pointing out that you've come to my rescue, which you have, twice now. Plus, she didn't have time to continue quizzing me because Bruce was due any minute."

"What'll you tell her as we continue to spend more time together on this case?"

"About that? Is there any way we can discover who killed Elliot today?"

"The sooner, the better, but we're so far off base right now, our culprit would almost have to walk right up to us and confess for us to solve this today. Why the rush?"

She made a face. "I made a coffee date with Pete Gordon for tomorrow morning. He said he had some inside knowledge about Elliot, but he didn't want to be seen talking very long with me at the party."

"Is that the only data you came away with from the party?" he asked.

"Yes, isn't it enough? Although my lech radar didn't go off, I was getting certain vibes from him."

"What kind of vibes?"

Rex could ask follow-up questions too. "Like he wanted to be seen with a television star," she replied.

He had the effrontery to laugh. "Who wouldn't, Marla?"

"Not you. You've done everything in your power to reduce the time we spend together, and even then, it's in your condo, away from everyone else."

"Don't throw this back on me. I'm your partner. Even if I

were attracted to you, we can't afford to complicate our mission with a relationship right now."

She'd never experienced such a logical rejection. Despite its making sense, for some odd reason, it was a bit of a letdown. "Don't worry about sparing my feelings."

He blinked. "Surely you haven't been thinking otherwise?"

"Of course not!" she rushed to say. "You just surprised me by saying it out loud."

"Let's try out that idea you mentioned earlier and analyze his credit-card charges."

twelve

· · ·

They downloaded Elliot's credit-card charge data onto a spreadsheet on her laptop. They laid it out by date starting with the approximate time Elliot moved into his condo back in January. There were charges every week, some weeks showing more entries than others. She printed off a separate report for Rex to analyze while she studied her own.

"It appears there were five periods of heaviest usage," she said after isolating the largest clusters of charges. "Early February, early April, mid-May, July and recently."

"And within each of those periods there are restaurant and motel charges," he said.

"There are restaurant charges throughout," she said, "but those in the five periods I mentioned appear to be more expensive places than the other restaurant charges, suggesting he was attempting to charm his dinner partner. The other charges were for less expensive meals, frequently for just one person and delivered rather than served in-house."

"You're suggesting those five periods were the times the Condo Casanova was in business," he said, following up on her theory.

She had to smile. Typically somber Rex Alcorn had made a funny. "Condo Casanova? Where did that come from?"

He pointed to his noggin. "What? You doubt my originality?"

"No. Just surprised by it."

"Anyway, I think your point about those five periods is a good one. At least a notion we can get our arms around and see how it pans out."

"Then our next step is to figure out who he would've been cozying up to. I think I can put names with three of the periods, but at this point this is pure speculation."

"You already have three names? Why haven't you shared this with me until now?" he asked in an accusatory tone. So much for their new fake relationship.

"We've just started our partnership. I'm ready to share now."

He gave her a look that said, "Let's stop playing games and get down to business." Aloud, he said, "Tell me what you know."

"To placate Kitty in her attempts to get me out of the condo to meet some of her friends, I went with her to her book club on Monday. I had already met Scottie Richards when I first arrived. I also met Kaitlin Fargo, who I now know was one of Elliot's neighbors, and Rita Haley, who Damien Chutney told me Elliot asked about several months back."

"Scottie Richards, Kaitlin Fargo and Rita Haley. So far, their only connection to the case is that they live in this building. What else have you got?"

"Scottie came to me before Patty Goodhue set up the dinner meeting with her husband. As you saw in the case notes, she was one of the first persons of interest the police visited the very morning of Elliot's death. Scottie claimed she had nothing to do with it and appealed to me to investigate and clear her name."

Rex held out the spreadsheet. "The case notes indicate she was his dinner guest in this recent period of credit card charges.

They only learned her identity because someone at one of the restaurants remembered her name."

"That probably was the night she refused for the second time his suggestion she invest in some project he was backing. He stormed out of the restaurant and left her to pay the bill," she replied.

"Did she tell you about her relationship with him?"

"Yes, although she didn't want to admit to the full extent of it at first. She's been a widow for a few years. She's seen other men socially, but there was more to the time she spent with Elliot than the others, brief as it was. She stayed overnight with him at local motels more than once, but it was only near the end of that time, about two weeks ago, he began hitting her up to invest."

Rex folded his hands and brought them up to his chin.

"What are you thinking?" she asked.

He squinted as if running an idea through his head one more time before sharing it with her. "This is just a theory. Theories are helpful when you're looking for answers to matters where there are few facts. But if we get too carried away with this one, we're in danger of taking ourselves into left field."

"Okay, okay. Your warning is clear. We won't jump to conclusions. What's your theory? Spill."

"Drake Elliot appears to have made his living by preying upon single rich women. We don't know the extent of his takings other than he was able to pay his credit card charges. His bank accounts don't reveal any large influx of cash. If he was successful, which I suspect, he squirreled the money away somewhere else. Very few complaints have been lodged against him over the years. I'm guessing that's because his marks have been too humiliated to contact the police. What Scottie Richards admitted to you is the first solid evidence against him."

"But there's a catch. She didn't tell the police as much as she revealed to Kitty and me," Marla said. "And she doesn't know I'm telling you about her. In fact, the last thing I said to her was to keep what she'd asked me to do just amongst her, Kitty and me. I don't feel right proceeding further without her knowing you're now on the team too."

He closed his eyes briefly. "I get how you want to be transparent with her, but we run the risk of her denying everything she told you and Kitty if she learns I'm also on the case. She knows I'm a former police officer."

Without realizing it at first, she once again touched her necklace under her shirt. "But we have to explain your part in this because I made her and Kitty promise not to tell anyone else about what I was doing."

"Let's table talking to Scottie Richards a bit," he said. "Tell me about the other two women you think might have dated Elliot."

"Keep in mind, this is me filling in the blanks. At book club, Rita Haley mentioned how she'd seen Kaitlin Fargo running out to an unknown car one night last February. Kaitlin wouldn't admit to anything, but she got really huffy when Rita brought it up. That's as much as I know, but wouldn't it make sense that he'd start close to home first?"

He nodded. "Besides talking to Scottie, we need to add Kaitlin Fargo to the list," he said. "What about Rita Haley?"

"All I know about her is what Damien Chutney told me. Elliot questioned him about her after they'd shared the elevator with her sometime last winter. Chutney said Elliot had commented on the diamond bracelet she was wearing once it was just the two of them. Then he wanted to know her marital status, and Chutney told him she was a recent divorcee."

"And?"

"That's it. I told you my hunch was based on very little solid evidence, other than Rita stayed out of the discussion of Kaitlin and Scottie's love life when that topic was being batted around at book club. Which could mean nothing, or she didn't want to bring any attention to her own situation."

"Add her to the list. Anyone else?"

"Isn't that enough for now?" she asked. "How do we approach them? We can't very well tell these women we're working with the police."

"Good question." His folded hands came down to his lap. "As the newcomer in the complex, would it be plausible for you to just drop by to get to know them better?"

She took a moment to consider how that might pan out. "I don't know, Rex. I can barely picture what I'd say, but how would I explain your presence? It's one thing to announce we're suddenly a couple but another to start asking questions about the murder."

"No idea. What else can you use?"

She'd been playing around with an idea in her head, but to activate it meant going against the very thing she'd been trying to do since she arrived in Minnesota: forget she was an out-of-work actress. But it seemed to be the only scenario she could come up with.

"What?" Rex asked. "Your eyes tell me something's cooking in there. Share."

"It's still half-baked."

"Run it by me. Maybe I can help with the other half."

"I stay as close to the truth as I can, which is, I'm an actress looking for a new project. I think there's a story in Elliot's murder, but I need more information."

"Good start. But why go to them for more information?" he asked.

"That's the unformed part. I need your help to flesh it out."

He held up a hand. "Whoa! I offered to help, but what you've described is outside my wheelhouse."

"Didn't you ever have to go undercover where you had to make up a story as you went?"

"No, ma'am. I was a law-and-order type. I kept the peace. But I didn't do any playacting. Taking on the role of your new boyfriend will be challenge enough."

What did he mean by that? Whatever, this wasn't the time to clarify his statement.

"Then I need time to work this through. I can't talk to them until I have a clearer idea how to even begin."

"Let's start with Scottie Richards," he said. "She's already on record with you. The only new script is how I play into this."

"Okay. Maybe she'll tell us something that will help pave the way with the other three. Give me a few minutes. I need to catch up with Kitty."

thirteen

. . .

Scottie broke into a wide smile when she saw it was Marla at her door. "Please tell me you have good news." Then she saw Rex, who'd stood to the side of the door. "Oh, hi, Rex. Why are you here?"

"May we come in?" Marla asked.

"I, uh, sure," Scottie replied. She glanced directly at Rex. "What's up?"

"Ask Marla," he replied.

Scottie turned back to Marla, eyes raised. "Okay. I'll bite. What brings the two of you to my place?"

Marla plunged ahead. "The more I thought about what I'd agreed to do for you, the more I realized how much I'd taken on. I need help. So I approached Rex and asked him to team up with me."

Scottie stared back at her. And then comprehension clicked. "Good grief! Are you telling me Rex knows?"

Rex caught his cue. "I couldn't believe she agreed to play investigator again when she first told me. She's been so adamant about leaving that part of her life in LA behind. But as it sunk in, we both realized bringing me on board had its advantages."

"Really? Do tell," Scottie said. "Adding a retired cop to the mix should be quite edifying."

Marla kept her tone even. "I don't know about 'edifying,' but Rex's background and his logical approach to problem-solving will go a long way toward figuring out who killed Drake Elliot. I told you from the start I wasn't a real investigator, but he was."

Scottie shook her head. "I can't believe you, Marla. The last thing you said the other day when you agreed to help me was to keep our 'arrangement' just between Kitty, you and me, and then you go back on your own words."

"That's why we're here now," Marla returned. "At the time, I had good reason for insisting we keep my task just among the three of us. Kitty needed to hear it, because I couldn't be sure she wouldn't be tempted to share our story with others. That still goes. But then Rex came on the scene, and, well, I felt we could benefit from his involvement."

"Now that we've brought you up to speed," Rex said, "let's get back to the case. Unless you'd prefer to release Marla from her commitment and let the chips fall where they may?"

Scottie's face puckered up. "I'm not happy about you coming on board, Rex, but what's done is done. I still want Marla, and now you, to find the killer and exonerate me." She sat back and folded her hands in her lap. "So, what have you learned?"

"We suspect Elliot approached others for money," Marla said.

"Who? Although there's a lot of speculation amongst all the scuttlebutt I've been hearing, no one else has come forth," Scottie said. "And why would they, unless the police got to them also?"

"I haven't wanted to draw undue attention to my promise to look into the case," Marla said. "So I went to the singles wine and cheese party last night and attempted to learn more about Elliot from individual residents simply as a newcomer attempting to understand how the murder affected people in the building. I talked to Damien Chutney and Pete Gordon."

"Good! You already learned about that singles group. I attended a few of their parties but never seemed to meet anyone I'd care to date. Did you learn anything from those folks?"

"Keep in mind, I don't have the same authority for asking questions as the police. My questions have to be couched in curiosity and the spirit of problem-solving. Even with Rex participating, we can't just put people on the spot."

"In other words, this is going slower than I'd like," Scottie said, picking up on Marla's caution.

"Yes, but we have learned a few things. For instance, as you probably suspected, you don't appear to be the first person in the complex Elliot approached for money."

Scottie's eyes widened. "Did they fall for his scheme? I wondered where the money was coming from to pay for our fancy dinners."

"We don't know that yet. There don't appear to be any major influxes of cash into his bank account since he moved into the building. I wanted to update you, especially about Rex's participation, before talking to these other potential victims of his scams."

"How did you gain access to his financial records?" she asked.

"You don't want to know," Rex told her.

She eyed him, and then a knowing smile crossed her face. "Having you on board, Rex, may prove beneficial after all."

He nodded but didn't reply.

"Anyway," Marla continued, "we're off to visit these people who might have been taken in by the guy. Before we do, though, have you remembered anything more about your dealings with him? Or have you heard more about him from anyone else?"

Scottie thought a moment. "Is Kaitlyn Fargo on your list of

possible victims? She came to see me the day after book club to apologize for commenting about my 'love life' to the group. I told her not to worry. Whatever had been going on in my private life was over and done with. At that point, she made a face, the kind you make when you accidentally taste sour milk, and said we appeared to have that in common. When I tried to pursue her comment, she downplayed her statement, just saying it wasn't easy being alone and nearing sixty and that at our age we had to watch ourselves so we didn't make bad choices."

"Did you mention Drake Elliot?" Rex asked.

"No. That was before the murder. At that point, he was the last person I wanted to talk about. But her comment about 'bad choices' could mean she gave him money. She's been divorced several years. From what I know about her finances, she lives comfortably, although I've never heard her described as filthy rich."

"Anything else?" Marla asked.

"The first few times I went out with Drake, he insisted I meet him at the restaurant. I was so flattered to be asked out by him, I agreed. For the first two dates anyhow. When he asked me out a third time, I told him I thought it was ridiculous we should go separately when we lived in the same building. He finally relented but only after I agreed to be picked up out front and not be seen meeting him in the garage. When I asked why the secrecy, he said it added to the ambience of our dates. I bought that line until he pressed too hard for money. Then I realized he didn't want any of the other women or men in the complex to catch on to his schemes.

"What I didn't tell you because I hadn't really thought about it at the time was that he wasn't just attempting to keep our dates a secret from everyone else in the building. As we drove away each time, he'd been looking in the rearview mirror and wouldn't even talk to me until we were a couple blocks away."

"He was afraid of being followed?" Rex asked.

"That's the way it seems to me now, after the fact. Does that help?"

Having never met Drake Elliot, Marla wasn't sure if the rearview mirror thing meant anything or not. He could've been a very cautious person. She glanced at Rex.

"It could," Rex said. "Thanks for letting us know."

"KAITLIN NEXT?" Rex asked as they left Scottie's.

"If she's home. If not, then Elliot's place," she said.

"Okay, meet me down there. I need to make arrangements with the building manager to get into there. Goodhue should've called to give his approval by now."

She used his absence to bring Kitty up to speed with a quick text.

Rex and I are on our way to interview Kaitlin Fargo about the murder. I'll explain about Rex when I see you. We needed a cover story, so we're telling her and whoever else we talk to that I'm involved because I want the rights to the story to use for a new project. We'll talk later.

She had just finished texting when Rex met her in the hallway leading to Kaitlin's condo.

"Let's see if Kaitlin Fargo is home first. If she's out, we do Elliot's condo first."

fourteen

. . .

"Hi, Kaitlin. I wonder if Rex and I could have a few minutes of your time," Marla said once Kaitlin came to the door.

"Uh, it's Marla, isn't it? And Rex? I'm surprised to see you here. Come in. Would you like some coffee?"

"None for either one of us. We shouldn't be long," Marla said as she and Rex headed for one of two sofas facing each other. A quick glance around their surroundings showed a tastefully done cream and coffee living room.

"Okay? What can I help you with?" Kaitlin said once she settled into the brown leather club chair opposite them.

"Like I told everyone at book club earlier in the week, I'm between projects. I've been actively seeking something as my next role. The recent murder of our fellow resident Drake Elliot has me interested. I think it would make a great limited series for me. I'd play a newcomer to the building whose sister is accused of the murder and she prevails upon me to prove her innocence."

"Oh, my God, have the police accused Kitty?" Kaitlin asked.

"No, sorry to give you that impression. What I have in mind would be a fictional adaptation based on this true story. I've asked Rex to help me with my research, since he's a former officer of the law and we've kinda clicked since I first met him."

Kaitlin glanced from Marla to Rex but didn't comment on that last part. "Okay, I follow you so far," Kaitlin replied. "Where do I come in?" she asked innocently.

"First, you were his next-door neighbor. Since he lived here less than a year and from all accounts appears to have stuck mainly to himself, we thought you could fill us in with what you know about him."

"Me? I hardly saw him either."

"Oh? You never ran into him in the corridor or elevator or garage?" Marla asked.

"Well, yes, on occasion, but that was just to say hi or talk about the weather. I can't complain about noise coming from his place."

"I'm pretty sure he was the driver of the car Sally Cunningham saw you getting into back in February. In fact, from what we've learned talking to others in the building, that was probably just one of the times you went out with him. You were having an affair with him. Is that correct?"

Kaitlin's complexion reddened and her eyes bulged. "Where? How? No one supposedly knew about us."

"Since we've gotten that far, let me tell you something else. It was brief, though we're guessing quite, uh, passionate, because you stayed overnight at different motels with him at least four times."

"How could you possibly ..." She took in Rex at that point. "Of course. Rex still has friends on the force. Did you check my bank account, too?"

"Not yet," Rex replied. "We hoped you'd tell us about your finances. Did you give him money?"

She started to say something, then closed her mouth. Instead, she rose and began charging about the room as if searching for her answer somewhere in the woodwork.

At length, she swirled around. "If I tell you about the money, will you believe I didn't kill him?"

Marla and Rex exchanged looks. "Okay, try us," Marla said.

"Shortly after he moved into the building last winter, he stopped by to introduce himself. Attempting to be a good neighbor, I invited him to dinner that night, which he accepted. He was quite charming then. Asked a lot of questions about me and my life. That night, I thought his interest in me was special. I openly told him about my ex-husband. It's been years since my divorce, but I gained a large settlement. Over the two bottles of wine he brought, I must have revealed more than was prudent about my financial situation."

"How long before he started suggesting you invest?" Rex asked her.

"That first night, although it was indirect. Just statements like, 'You should look into ...' But two days later he was back at my door asking me out to dinner that night to repay my hospitality. Even then, he simply asked if I'd had a chance to check out the investment opportunity he'd recommended.

"His questions about my finances escalated the more I saw him. That was my fault. I should have cut things off with him early on, but he made me feel so special when he'd take me to dinner, I couldn't bring myself to say no, especially after we, you know. It had been a long time since I'd been with a man. Once you're with someone again, it's difficult to stop. But it soon became clear, if our liaison was to continue, I needed to put some money into one of the so-called opportunities he'd been talking about. Incessantly."

"Didn't it seem to you that you were ..." Marla started to ask.

"Paying for his services?" Kaitlin said. "Only since then. At the time, I was desperate to keep him in my life, especially once he started hinting he might turn his attentions elsewhere."

"What did you invest in?" Rex asked.

"A parcel of land south of town which doesn't exist. At least it wasn't really for sale. I didn't discover that until the next month when he'd moved on to his next victim. Yes, by then I realized he'd been nothing more than a con man."

"Did you try to get the money back from him?" Rex asked.

Her hands went to her hips. "I confronted him all right. The same day I learned my investment was worth nothing. He gave me this perplexed expression and said there had to be some mistake. He didn't offer to fix things or even apologize. In fact, I didn't see much of him after that, other than a few times when we hit the elevator at the same time. And then he acted like we'd never met."

"Did you go to the police with your complaint?" Marla asked.

"To the police?" For the first time since they'd been there, her voice rose. "What would they have been able to do? I voluntarily put my money in that account. And it would have created a public record, the last thing I wanted."

"That's what he was counting on," Marla said. "You didn't want your friends here in the building to know you'd been duped."

Kaitlin didn't respond other than to stare down at her hands.

"I'm sorry he took you for so much money," Marla said, not knowing the exact amount, "but because you kept silent, others probably lost money too."

Their hostess continued gazing at her hands. "I didn't think of that." Her voice had lost its ferocity and gone quite soft.

Rex took his turn. "Instead, you continued to live next door to him for another six months, your anger and guilt mounting day by day until you finally couldn't live with it anymore. Thus, he couldn't continue to live. You arranged to meet him out by the pond in the middle of the night, offered him more money, and when he wasn't looking, you killed him."

Her eyes shot wide open, and she came out of her seat. "No! You've got it all wrong. True, I hated the man. But if I was going to get even with him, I would have done it months ago so I wouldn't have to see him every day. Or at least know he was still operating out of the condo next door."

"How much did you say you lost?" Marla asked again.

"I didn't. Does it even matter now? There's no way I can get it back."

Rex persisted. "How much?"

"Twenty thousand," she said in such a low voice, Marla wasn't sure she'd heard.

"That's a lot of money," Marla said.

"Surely that knowledge grinds against your better judgment every day," Rex said.

"Yes, it does. But killing him wouldn't have made the pain go away, and I would have paid even dearer if I'd done it and been caught."

Once again, Marla and Rex exchanged glances.

Marla took the lead. "Okay, if you didn't kill him, you need to help us find out who did."

Kaitlin didn't take her seat again, but she did return to lean against it. "Help you? How?"

"Like I told you earlier, with Rex's help, I'm attempting to make sense out of this murder. Besides finding the killer, I want to adapt the story to a project of some sort. In order to do that, we need to discover who else might've been taken in by him. We need names from you."

"Names? You think I've shared my story with others?"

"Have you?" Rex asked her outright.

"No!"

"But you're in the best position to guess," Marla pointed out. "Your radar has to have gone off the chart once you learned you couldn't trust him."

"You're wrong. I don't know anything."

Rex had shared a technique with her to be used only if they ran out of other methods to get her to talk. It was time to apply it now.

She settled farther back on the couch and clasped her hands in her lap. And didn't speak.

Rex, picking up on her cue, did the same.

Their silent act went on for some time. Marla had begun to doubt this approach when Kaitlin finally broke.

"Scottie Richards."

"Good, that's something," Rex said.

"We already know about Scottie," Marla told her.

"Then I can't help you."

"Think it through. Surely you've noticed someone else demonstrating the same behavior as you a few months earlier? Besides you and Scottie, we think there were at least three more victims."

"He did keep busy," Kaitlin said.

"So?" Rex asked.

"Maybe Rita Haley," she said, as if questioning herself. "She's recently divorced. Remember how we commented on her hefty settlement at book club? I don't know anything for sure, but she would have been ripe for the plucking. Oh. Sorry. Even I don't have a right to describe it like that."

"We got the picture, though," Rex said.

"What about your sister?" Kaitlin asked.

"What about Kitty?" Marla asked, afraid she'd hear something she didn't want to hear.

"She's been on her own for years. And she has a considerable nest egg. Those seem to be the two top qualifications to have caught Elliot's attention."

"Kitty wasn't involved with him," Marla said.

"Don't be so sure, Marla. Kitty has been known to be gullible at times."

"I don't disagree," Marla replied. "But apparently her attention has been held the last few months by Roger Halliwell."

"She couldn't have been with him twenty-four seven. If Elliot had shown the least interest in her, she would have found some way to deal with them both."

"We'll keep that in mind," Rex said. "Any other names come to mind?"

"Good grief, I went from no names to three. Isn't that enough?"

"Not if you've thought of more."

"I haven't. But if you'll leave me alone, maybe more will occur to me. I'm not promising, but the well is dry now."

"Okay, Kaitlin. Thank you," Marla said, rising.

Out in the hall once the door had closed on them, she turned to Rex. "I wish we'd gotten more, but at least we have confirmation of our suspicions."

"Better than I thought we'd get," he said. "And she seemed to buy your story about why the questions."

"The next time should be easier."

"You threw me for a second. But I like the idea of your asking questions as a stepping stone to your next project."

"I feel like I'm letting myself down, returning to my role as an investigator to explain the questions. I vowed I wouldn't do anything like Letitia Carruthers again. But it was the first thing I came up with."

"If the investigator thing bothers you so much, how about

switching it up a bit? Say you're researching the Elliot case to be part of your own podcast. They've become popular."

She gazed at him with new interest. "That's a great suggestion."

"Careful," he said, a smile creeping onto his face. "You might be starting to like me."

fifteen

. . .

"Time to check out Elliot's place," Rex said once they'd left Kaitlin's condo.

"Did the building manager give you access to his entry code?"

"Not quite." He texted something. "The building manager will be here in two minutes."

She shot him a look of surprise. "I thought Goodhue said he'd clear entry for us?"

"He did, but apparently the building manager is concerned about their liability if they share the code, even if the police give their official permission for us to be in there."

"She knows we're working for the police?"

"Not investigating. The story he gave was that he'd asked me, as a retired officer, to check out Elliot's quarters so as not to upset the other building residents."

"And she believed that?"

"Partially," Rex replied.

"How do we explain my presence?"

Rex tilted his head to the side. "We don't, unless she asks."

"And if she does?"

"I'll leave that to you. You did quite well explaining our mission to Kaitlin. I trust you'll come up with something just as plausible."

Great. She was becoming increasingly unenthused with the tasks her *partner* kept dumping on her. Her best hope was that the manager, Gretchen Sanstrom, wouldn't ask why she was there. To that end, Marla would act like she had every right to be there and not offer an explanation unless pressed.

To their surprise, Sanstrom sent her assistant, Iris Cadell, to observe their efforts. Cadell showed up within two minutes of Rex's text, explaining that Sanstrom had gone home with a bad migraine. A tall, slender woman with dark red hair, Cadell reminded Marla of the head resident of her dorm when she was a freshman in college: aloof and unapproachable. "Mr. Alcorn," she said as she came up to Elliot's door. Then she saw Marla. "And you are?"

"Marla Dane," Marla borrowed from her best Letitia all-knowing voice. She extended her hand. "I'm Kitty Lovejoy's sister, visiting from California."

"I don't recall it being mentioned that you would be joining us."

Damn! As much as she kept trying to keep Letitia in her past, this murder case kept forcing her to revert. At the moment, though, Letitia was her best option. "I don't know if you've heard of me, but I'm an actress fresh off six seasons playing a private investigator, Letitia Carruthers. I've been considering several possibilities as my next project, and then this 'incident' with Mr. Elliot happened. It seemed like the perfect next step for me, to make the solving of his case the subject of a new project. So I prevailed on Rex to bring me in on things."

That explanation had more holes in it than her last pair of pantyhose, and it didn't totally satisfy the assistant building manager. "I've heard you are a former police officer, Mr. Alcorn, but that still doesn't explain why you're here and not the police."

"Suffice it to say, the chief needed another pair of eyes to check out this condo and asked me to do it," Rex replied, offering no further explanation.

The authority in his tone appeared to satisfy their observer. "We're waiting on the condo's owner to decide when to bring in a new tenant. The police must release the unit first," Cadell said, showing them in after entering the code in the keypad.

"Have you heard from the next of kin?" Rex asked.

"No, not yet. We'll leave it up to the owner to determine how to dispose of Mr. Elliot's belongings. There aren't many."

Hopefully they could learn more about Elliot's friends and relatives by searching his digs. As long as Cadell wasn't watching over their shoulders.

"Perhaps you'd like to take a seat while we work through his rooms?" Marla asked.

"I'm supposed to observe wherever you go and whatever you do and report back to Gretchen," she said. "But, thanks, I'll make myself comfortable on his sofa while you're in this room."

That should be fun. They let her settle and then they moved off to themselves.

"Where do we start?" Marla asked.

"Anywhere that looks like it might hold documents or information," he replied. "The police already took his notepad computer. Analysis showed very little of interest on it. They downloaded the contents into an online file."

Now he told her. She could've been reading through that file before they started their explorations this morning. Too late now.

There was no desk in the room, but there was a large drawer under the library table. Empty. The lone bookcase held about twenty books. Marla and Rex took turns removing each and fanning them open for secret contents. Again nothing.

Nothing in the drawers in the entertainment center except a listing of TV programs.

A search behind and under the cushions of the sofa sectional, after they asked Cadell to move, netted them a quarter and a single dollar bill plus assorted popcorn kernels, candy bar wrappers and a comb. They gifted those to her.

In the kitchen they found several menus from various local restaurants in a cabinet drawer.

The refrigerator revealed a large collection of takeaway boxes, neatly stacked and marked. The freezer held several frozen meals but no notes or other treasures.

They next searched the main bedroom. Cadell followed along and leaned against the door, watching. Either a housekeeper visited every so often or Elliot had been just that neat. The bed was made. All his clothes were either put away or in the laundry basket in his walk-in closet. His wardrobe was skimpy but filled with high-quality shirts, slacks, sports jackets and two suits.

When they found nothing extraordinary with the obvious, they turned their attention to the more offbeat, starting first under the mattress. Nothing. Probably too obvious for the non-obvious.

Then they looked under the bed and the bottom of the mattress. Those were great spots for hiding things. Apparently Elliot hadn't thought so.

Behind the headboard? No.

Underneath the bureau drawers? No.

"Let's try his walk-in closet again," Marla told Rex.

Cadell moved further into the room. Sanstrom would be so pleased with her assistant's devotion to duty.

They went through every pocket of his pants, shirts, jackets and suits and came up with zero. Then they examined every corner of the carpet. It was tacked down everywhere. No place to slip anything under it. Rex climbed a stepstool they found in a kitchen closet and felt every spot along the top of the shelf that ran above the clothing rod.

Marla sank onto a corner of the bed. "I was so sure if we did find something, it would be somewhere here in the main bedroom. But unless you can think of a place we've missed in here, I say we move on."

"We're down to the guest bedroom and the bathrooms," Rex said.

"Let's try the main bath while we're here," Marla said. "Did you want to join us in here, Ms. Cadell?" she called.

Cadell came to the bathroom door. "I'll wait right outside."

"Thank God," Rex said once they were out of Cadell's hearing. "I'd hoped Gretchen would oversee our efforts instead of the attentive Iris Cadell. So be it. Don't share any more than you have to with her. God knows what she'd do with the information."

"I figured that out for myself," Marla replied. "How it is you're on a first-name basis with Gretchen Sanstrom?"

Rex acted like he hadn't heard her question. He went first to the tank and removed the lid. "Damn, used to find drug stashes in here in the old days"

"Did you or do you have something going with Gretchen Sanstrom?" Marla asked again.

"The staff aren't supposed to fraternize with residents," Rex finally said. "Otherwise ... who knows?"

"But you might have otherwise?"

"Why so curious about my private life, Dane?"

Why was she curious about his relationship with the building manager? "We're partners. I should know if you've got something going with one of the staff." She stopped short of telling him such a connection could be helpful.

They moved on to the linen closet. It also disappointed them.

That left the medicine cabinet. Not much to see there, either. An expensive brand of men's shampoo, the same brand of hair conditioner, styling gel for men, hairspray, a small leatherbound manicure set, a razor and a bottle of painkillers. She was about to close the door when she noticed a tiny paper triangle emerging from under the mirror. "We may have found something, Rex." She pointed to the paper. "All I have to do is figure out how to remove it without tearing it."

He briefly studied what she'd found and then reached over her shoulder and removed the manicure kit. It took more than a little finesse to dislodge it without tearing it, but he was finally successful. Having a trained police officer on the job was paying off.

She started to exclaim when he put a finger to his mouth. "No need to alert Ms. Cadell. At least now. Take a picture of this with your phone."

She did as directed, not quite sure why the secrecy.

He held it up for them both to read at the same time. It was a list of names, dates and amounts. Kaitlin Fargo, as "Fargo," was the first name with the date of February 17, $20K. Next came a name they didn't recognize, Tansy with the date of March 25, $35K. After that, Haley, May 18, $50K. Those names were followed by Richards, Donnelly, and Walker, with a blank next to each of them. A hundred and five thousand in less than six months.

"Now we have proof he was conning these folks as well as three more names," Rex said.

To Marla's relief, the name Lovejoy wasn't on the list. Not even as a possible future mark as those three with the question marks must have been. "Looks like I'm keeping my coffee date with Gordon Peters tomorrow, although I got the impression from him that he knew of another resident who'd been affected, not him."

"That may have been his way to tell you about his own folly."

Rex attempted to stick the note back in the cabinet, but it wouldn't go in. Foiled on that account, he pulled a plastic bag from his jeans pocket and inserted the paper. Then he stuck the bag inside his shirt.

"I take it we're keeping our discovery to ourselves," she said in a lowered voice.

"Yeah. I'll explain later."

She picked up the manicure kit, still unzipped, and played a finger around the binding. "Hand me those tweezers." She inserted just the tip in the top of the binding and closed the two prongs against something she felt inside. A tiny piece of paper, about a third of the size of the list they'd just found, emerged. This one merely said 982504-1.

She showed it to Rex. "Any idea what this is?" she asked.

"Could be a lot of things," Rex responded. "A code. Part of a telephone number. A confirmation number of some sort. Maybe even a bank number."

"None of that information will help us ID the killer."

"But Goodhue might appreciate it." He took a picture and sent it off to the police chief. "The decoding specialist might be able to use it to track the money. Because we now have proof he conned those people. We have a motive."

"Speaking of which," she said, "as soon as we're done here, we should talk to Rita Haley, since Elliot's notes indicate he got the most from her."

"Good idea, except she might've been in a better position to lose all that money than one of those who lost less, since her divorce settlement supposedly left her quite wealthy."

"Are we done here since we've found those two pieces of evidence?"

He rubbed the back of his neck. "Probably should finish up completely, just so we can feel secure we covered it all."

She would've preferred to move on immediately to Rita Haley, now that they had an idea how much she lost, but Rex was the expert here. She'd follow his lead.

"We're almost done, Ms. Cadell," Rex called to the assistant manager as they left the main bath and headed to the guest room. Cadell followed and immediately lighted in the over-stuffed easy chair. They repeated the same checks as in the main bedroom: between the mattress and bed springs, under the mattress, under the bed, behind the headboard, etc. Still nothing.

"Why would he hide something in here on the off chance a guest might find it?" Marla asked at length.

"Good point, except I doubt he ever had any guests, which would possibly make this room the best hiding place."

She couldn't argue that point.

The closet, less extensive than in the main bedroom, revealed nothing. In fact, there was nothing in there other than a few hangers on the clothes pole.

The bathroom came up empty also. Nothing in that medicine cabinet.

That left only the linen closet. It contained two sets of bath towels, hand towels, washcloths and a bath mat. They ran their fingers between each folded item. As a last-ditch effort, Marla stuck her fingers inside the two bath towels. In the second, she struck gold, or at least a folded-up newspaper from six months prior.

"Check to see where our monitor is," Rex whispered to her.

Marla peeked out the door. "Still seated, but her eyes are directed on us," she whispered back.

He stuck the newspaper inside his shirt. "Can you see it under here?" he asked.

"Yes, because I know it's there. What if you stuck it behind your shirt and down your pants?"

"I would if I could," he replied. "Help me."

"Huh?"

He lifted the back of his shirt with one hand while he still held the newspaper in his other. "Stick it several inches past my waistband and then place the back of my shirt over the rest."

Easier said than done. Rex wore his pants tight. Propping them open enough to insert part of the paper meant she had to pry a few fingers inside his waistband and touch skin. Warm skin. She closed her eyes briefly, even though she should've kept them open the whole time to make sure nothing was exposed. What was going on with her? No time right now to figure it out.

"Thanks," Rex said in a slightly husky voice when she'd finished.

"Yeah, right," she replied, unable to think of a better response.

"Looks like we're done here," Rex told Cadell when they came out of the bathroom. His voice had returned to its usual brusque tone.

"The police did a pretty thorough search the same day as his death. They took away quite a few items."

Without prior discussion, they both hung their heads. "And now we've reassured ourselves that was the case," Rex replied submissively. "Thank you for taking the time to appease us."

They said goodbye to Iris Cadell in the corridor but hung around Elliot's condo until she was out of sight.

"Let's take the steps up to my place to check out what we found," Rex said.

Fortunately, they didn't run into anyone on the way up. Rex was able to remove the newspaper on his own, so she was spared having to touch him again. Good news or bad news? She wasn't sure.

They spread the newspaper out on the island in Rex's kitchen. Rex quickly flipped through it, page by page. "Nothing marked or highlighted," he said.

"There must be something significant in it or he wouldn't have kept it. He didn't hold on to anything else. Let's take it page by page starting with page one."

The newspaper was from a small city in Illinois. The day's big headline was the announcement that a major social media outlet planned to build a data farm just outside town. "Now there's a perfect investment opportunity," Rex said. "But there appears to have been quite a bit of due diligence conducted. I don't see how he could've had his claws in it."

They studied the interior pages closely, but nothing sparked their interest. Nor did the ads. The death announcements and obituaries held nothing.

Rex was about to turn the page when Marla spotted a short article announcing that one of a team of con artists, who had been caught, tried and judged guilty, was about to start a three-year prison sentence that day. She would've gone right past it except for the word "con" in the small headline.

The subject of the article had been convicted of a fake life insurance scam in a bunch of nursing homes. He'd apparently convinced a number of residents to buy life insurance that would supposedly double and go to their children on their death. Unfortunately, this kind of thing went on all too often despite the efforts of nursing home officials to protect their people. Marla would've moved on to another article except the last sentence said the man's partner had never been caught.

"Rex? Take a look at this." She pointed to the article. "Is it possible the partner they mention was Drake Elliot?"

"Do you want to call Goodhue or should I?"

"Me? I thought you were his contact here in the building?"

"I've already forwarded the list of names and takings and that strange number to him. It's your turn."

"Okay. As soon as we've talked to Rita Haley," she said.

"And Marla?"

"Yes?"

"Don't get too excited about that article. He saved that newspaper for some reason, or he wouldn't have tucked it inside a folded towel. But that may have been for another reason. Maybe nothing more than the mention of a name he wanted to remember."

"Got it." She'd known as much. She wished Rex hadn't felt the need to warn her not to get her hopes up, but he seemed to think part of his role in this partnership was to guide her and keep her from going off track.

Maybe Rita Haley would shed the light they'd been seeking.

sixteen

. . .

"This is a surprise," Rita Haley said when she opened her door to Marla and Rex.

"A good one, we hope," Marla answered. "May we come in?"

"Uh, sure, but I need to leave for my exercise class in fifteen minutes. Have a seat. Why are you here?" she asked as soon as they were each sitting.

Though the same floor plan as Kitty's, Haley's condo was like an instantaneous trip to the Far East. The living room boasted rich red and black brocade furniture resting on a plush gold carpet. A large black teak cabinet with gold pulls and hinges occupied a place of honor along an interior wall. Along another wall, a low-boy cabinet, its gold sides painted with scenes from a wood, was topped with three brass tapers. Everything screamed recent makeover costing thousands.

Marla took her time deciding where to sit. She was afraid she might break something. "I think I mentioned at book club the other day that I was spending time in Minnesota with my sister while I looked for a new project. At the time, I didn't antic-ipate finding something so soon, but this recent murder of one of the residents has given me an idea. I want to turn the investigation into some sort of television project."

Haley settled in a chair facing them and waited expectantly. "I got the impression from your remarks at book club that you were quite done with the private eye genre. Anything to do with crime."

Marla nodded. "You remember correctly. But then this murder happened and I got to talking to Rex, who I learned was a former cop, and the next thing I knew, I was deep in an unofficial investigation. More like research."

"And I'm part of your *research*?"

The woman didn't pull any punches.

"Here's what we've learned so far. Ever since Drake Elliot moved into this building," Marla said, "he began wining and dining various single women who live here, insisting they meet him in private so no one else knew how many different women he was seeing. That part would've only made him a Lothario. But he also got some of these women to invest in various financial opportunities, and he wound up scamming them for over a hundred thousand dollars."

"And you're asking me what I know about all this?"

"That and more to the point, were you a victim of one of his scams?" Rex asked.

Rita's eyes revealed no surprise. "Why do you think he hit on me?"

"Months ago, you rode on the elevator with him and another resident. You were apparently wearing a diamond bracelet in which he showed interest to this other person. He then asked if you were married."

"That's it?"

"No," Marla said. "We've found evidence in his own handwriting that he got you for fifty thousand dollars."

They did their silent act again, waiting for Rita's reaction to that revelation.

Rita chewed a lip. And then, like the sudden burst of the rain shower earlier that week, she broke down. Tears poured down her face, even though she tried to stem them with her hands.

"Rita? Are you okay?" Marla asked, fishing a tissue out of her pocket.

"Do I look okay?" Rita returned through gulps, her face distorted by tears.

"No, of course not," Rex said. "If what happened to you is what we think happened, you have every right to break down."

Rita dabbed at her eyes with the tissue, but the flow continued.

Rex rose and went to the kitchen. He returned a minute later with a glass of water for her.

Rita sipped in between outbursts.

Now Marla rose and went in search of a box of tissues, since hers was long past its usefulness.

They waited some more.

After several more minutes, tissues, gulps and sips of water, Rita was finally ready to talk. "Everyone in the building thinks I'm richer than King Midas after my divorce settlement. That's mostly true. But I'm also paying for my granddaughter's education, since my daughter can't afford to. I don't consider myself susceptible to get-rich-quick schemes, but as I saw my funds draining away this past year, and she was only a freshman, I didn't dismiss Drake's suggestion I invest in his project out of hand. I didn't jump immediately, either.

"I should never have mentioned my concern that I couldn't pay for all four years of her college career, because he pounced on that motive and wouldn't let go. Then he added that I could double my investment. At that point, I couldn't resist."

Neither Marla nor Rex spoke right away.

"How did you learn he'd taken advantage of you?" Marla asked finally.

"My bank called, asking about the expenditure. By then, it had already gone through into whatever account he'd set up. They attempted to trace it with no success."

"Did you report him to the police?" Rex asked.

She hung her head. "I didn't tell anyone besides the people at my bank, even though they urged me to report him. I was so embarrassed at my foolishness. No, not embarrassed. Humiliated. I should've told people here and maybe prevented anyone else from being scammed, but I just couldn't bring myself to admit I'd let him take advantage of me. Everyone here thinks I'm so on top of things to have gotten so much money in my divorce settlement. I didn't want to burst that bubble. As it is, I'll soon need to tell my daughter I can no longer pay for all of my granddaughter's tuition. That breaks my heart."

There was little they could say to comfort her, but now they had to move to the even more difficult subject.

"Did you confront Elliot when you learned you'd been cheated?" Marla asked as a preliminary to the big question.

Rita blew out a huff. "You bet I did! He didn't open the door the first two times. But I was persistent and kept calling his name until he finally did let me enter. When I told him what my bank had told me, he claimed it would just take a little more time for the payment to process. Then he went on to say that even after it processed, I probably wouldn't see immediate results since this was a start-up operation. He never mentioned that aspect when he was singing the benefits of the opportunity and urging me to get on board as soon as I could."

"According to info we found in his condo, you invested in May. Did you take no action against him in the months since?"

"I started to. I called the bank to learn who I could contact to complain, but when they started to ask for the details, I hung up.

They made me feel like I was a child who'd gotten into trouble. And I didn't want the information getting back to my ex-husband. He couldn't take back the money, but he could try to turn my daughter against me."

Though Marla felt for her, she couldn't believe the woman could lose fifty thousand dollars without making more noise. But that seemed to be Elliot's MO. He must've developed a sixth sense when it came to selecting his victims and only hit upon those who wouldn't fight back. Maybe that's why nothing had ever developed between him and Kitty.

"All these months, you've probably been carrying a lot of fury around inside you," Marla said.

Rita narrowed her eyes like she suspected a trick question was coming. "Yes?"

"The more you thought about how you'd been duped, the more anger you felt. It continued to build until finally it snapped. You had to do something. You had to get back at him."

Rita's hand shot up. "Hold it! I didn't kill him, if that's where you're going."

Rex took a stab at getting her to crack. "But it would've been so easy. All you had to do was lure him down to the pond in the middle of the night. You'd already picked out the spot and how you'd do it. You could've ..."

"Stop! I hated him for what he'd done. But I wouldn't have gotten my revenge that way. I'd be in prison the rest of my life if I'd been found out. It's been bad enough losing the fifty thousand and my daughter and granddaughter's respect. I wouldn't want to give up my freedom the rest of my life just for a momentary release."

She sounded credible, but Marla suspected real murderers could sound sincere to the very end. On the show, they broke so easily once Letitia fingered them. She'd always thought they'd caved too easily due to the producers' desire to wrap the show quickly.

"What more do I have to do to convince you I didn't do it?" she asked, a distinctly plaintive note to her voice.

"It's just hard for us to believe you kept your anger and humiliation to yourself all this time," Marla said.

"What else could I have done, besides go to the police?"

"You could've talked to someone like a counselor," Rex said.

"A counselor would've told me to go to the police. I should know. I used to be one."

"Rita, that attitude is like representing yourself in court," Marla told her. "No matter how good you might be at the job, you still can't see the situation from anywhere but your own perspective."

Rita blew her nose before speaking again. "You're right. I just couldn't bring myself to tell another person what I'd done, no matter how trained they were for such situations."

"Which is what you just did with us," Rex said.

"Yes, I guess I did, but you didn't give me much choice."

Rex continued along that line. "So maybe that broke the ice enough for you to talk to someone now?"

She considered. "Maybe."

"Let's say we believe you," Marla said. "We need your help finding whoever did kill Elliot."

Her crying jag on hold, Rita narrowed her eyes. "Why did you say you're doing this? You're not a trained investigator, and Rex, you're no longer an active policeman."

"Like I said earlier, I've been looking for a new project since leaving *Carruthers on the Case*. I've been playing around with the idea of a limited series to executive produce. Or maybe I'd narrate a podcast featuring how an ordinary citizen helps the police solve a murder."

Haley rose. "Want some coffee? I feel the sudden need for caffeine."

They turned her down, then waited for her to return to the living room with her own mug.

"I was on the treadmill in the fitness room last month. I'm usually there late morning when no one else is around. But this one particular day I was joined by a woman I didn't recognize. She started up a conversation. I would have preferred to have been left alone, but I answered her questions as I could. She was new to the building and wanted to know about the people who lived here. Seemed innocuous enough, so I shared a little information about some."

"And Drake Elliot was one of those people?" Marla guessed.

"Yes. She didn't get around to him right away. She dropped his name into the mix after we'd talked about three or four others first."

"What did she want to know about him?" Rex asked.

"The usual things. Was he married? Was he seeing someone? What did he do for a living? Then finally, how long had he lived here? For some reason, that last one seemed out of kilter. It was a perfectly natural question, but it just didn't seem to fit with what she'd been asking about other residents. So I called her on it. She explained that he looked familiar and she wondered if she'd met him before coming here. It could have been that she was just curious, but it struck me as odd. Nevertheless, I put it in the back of my mind until you just asked."

"What made you remember it now?" Marla asked.

"The fact that she'd asked about Elliot."

"Who is this woman?" Rex asked.

"Her name is Donna Walker. She lives on the first floor."

"Have you seen her since that day in the fitness room?" Rex asked.

"No. Her lease shouldn't be up for several months yet, but

she seems to have disappeared from sight. I don't know if she ever connected with him or not, but she came to mind when you asked for my help."

There didn't seem to be much more they could learn from Haley, so they thanked her for her information.

"Don't forget to find yourself a counselor," Rex added as they left, touching her briefly on the shoulder.

"I'll think about it. Thank you for caring," she replied.

"Donna Walker. That last name was one of the blanks on Elliot's list," Marla said as they walked away from Rita Haley's condo. "Someone else to check out. But first, how 'bout lunch at Kitty's?"

seventeen

. . .

"Peanut butter and jelly or jelly and peanut butter?" Marla asked after surveying Kitty's kitchen for lunch items.

"Sorry to be an unappreciative guest," Rex replied, "but I'm allergic to peanut butter, and I don't particularly like jelly. Doesn't Kitty keep a large supply of yogurt in her fridge?"

"I had the last one yesterday. How about a can of soup?"

"How 'bout we go to my place?

"Seems like the two of you are spending a lot of time at Rex's condo the last few days," Kitty said from the door.

"We need to do a grocery run, my treat, Kitty," Marla said, ignoring her sister's remark. "I couldn't find anything in your larder to treat Rex to lunch, which is why he suggested we go to his place."

Kitty leaned against the doorjamb, a hand on her hip. "What's going on with you two? I ran into Scottie at the hairdresser a little while ago. She told me Rex is now helping you find Drake Elliot's killer when you're the one who made such a big deal about keeping your investigation on the QT amongst her, me and you."

"It made good sense to include Rex in my efforts since he's a retired cop. He's advising me."

Kitty turned to Rex. "I can't believe you're going along with this."

"She'd already committed to helping Scottie clear her name. What would you have had me do? Let her do this on her own?"

"Hey, guys. *She* is right here in front of you, and *she* isn't completely helpless. I just thought it prudent to enlist Rex's years of experience."

"I know that, Marla," her sister replied. "And if pressed, Rex would probably agree. It's just that all you told Scottie you'd do was *look into things*. And now it sounds like you're a full-blown detective, the very thing you've been trying to escape.?"

If only she could tell Kitty how she'd been pulled further into this case and assigned Rex as her partner by Chief Goodhue. But even if she could, she doubted Kitty would approve.

"I'm sorry you had to learn about Rex's involvement from Scotty and not me," Marla said. "But this all came together quickly. There wasn't time to catch you up, especially since

you've been otherwise engaged with Bruce Cranston."

Kitty waved her hand dismissively. "That's old news. Bruce and I went separate ways after I discovered he's only separated from his wife. For a couple years. I don't date married men."

"How about we update you now about what we've discovered thus far?" She watched Rex's reaction to make sure she hadn't gone too far.

"Good idea, Marla," Rex replied.

Thank goodness he recognized Kitty's need to feel involved. "To recap our morning, we started with Scottie to see if she might've remembered anything more about Drake Elliot. She mentioned how the guy always checked his rearview mirror when they pulled away from the building. Not the safety kind of thing, more the cautious, looking-over-his-shoulder-to-see-who-might-be-following-him kind of thing."

"Like someone from his past he wanted to avoid?" Kitty asked.

"Yeah, that kind of thing," Rex replied.

"Maybe he'd been scamming for years in other places and someone he duped came to find him," Kitty said.

"Maybe," Rex answered, "although as Drake Elliot he had a pretty clean police record."

"And that's a huge leap from him always checking his rearview mirror," Marla said.

"But it could mean you've been looking in the wrong place for suspects," Kitty replied. "Maybe his murderer didn't come from this condo complex at all."

Rex and Marla exchanged looks. Kitty had caught on fast, perhaps too fast. "But until we have more to go on from his past," Marla said, "we have to stay focused on Rambling Meadows, especially if that eliminates everyone from here."

"Who else did you talk to?"

"Kaitlin Fargo and Rita Haley," Marla replied. "We didn't get much new information from either, although they both finally admitted to having given him money and confronted him when they learned their investments weren't going anywhere. He just suggested something had gone wrong with the processing. He never admitted blame."

By tacit agreement, they didn't mention their search of his condo, which meant they didn't go into finding a sort of code and a list of his "donors."

"I am so glad I decided to pass on Drake Elliot," Kitty said.

"Did he ever approach you?" Rex asked.

"Early on. He invited me out to dinner one night back in January. It had been so cold and snowy up to then, I'd stayed in most of the time. Even had my groceries delivered. But that week the temps were in the thirties and a lot of the snow melted. I was anxious to get out, so I accepted his dinner invite with relish. We had a nice dinner complete with expensive wine. He kept encouraging me to drink up. When I stopped at two glasses, he tried to top me off with a third, which I refused. That's when my date radar kicked in. Without knowing him better, he simply could have been acting the good host, but on the other hand, I've learned to be leery of dates trying to ply me with alcohol."

"Was that your only date with him?" Marla asked.

"No, he asked me out two weeks later. My social life had tapered off after Christmas, so I gave him one more chance. Did I mention he was handsome and charming and he liked to ask questions and really listen to my answers, unlike a lot of dates I've had, who prefer to talk about themselves? Again, he ordered expensive wine and insisted I drink up. About that time, I started paying more attention to the kinds of questions he asked. I didn't bring you up, Marla, but apparently he'd heard from someone else about you, so he wanted to know all about your life in LA and your TV career. That's when the subject of money came up, starting with your money and how much you earned. When I shut him off there, it segued into my money and then my investment portfolio. Once again, my date radar kicked in, and I moved on to another topic. His whole persona changed about then, less friendly, less charming and ready to end the evening. Which was fine with me. I didn't hear from him after that night."

"Did you discuss him with anyone else in the building?" Rex asked.

"You mean, did I warn them to keep away from him? No. I could have, but I didn't think I'd be believed. The other single women would have dismissed whatever I told them about him as my attempt to keep him away from them."

"Do you know someone named Tansy?" Marla asked.

Kitty scrunched up her eyes. "Tansy? That name sounds familiar, but I can't place it immediately. Why do you ask?"

"We think he or she was another one of Elliot's victims," Rex said. "Now that we're talking about it, the name sounds familiar to me too. But like you, I can't think why."

"There's a couple frozen pizzas in the freezer you must have missed, if you want to stay for lunch," Kitty said.

Rex eyed Marla. Marla anticipated him. "Good idea. Maybe one of you will remember where you heard the name Tansy while we're heating one."

The mild sausage pizza, Kitty's favorite, turned out to be fairly tasty when teamed with the small garden salads Kitty made them. Neither Kitty nor Rex said much while they ate, their minds elsewhere.

Finally, Rex put down his half-eaten third slice. "Mind if I make a phone call? You can listen in, or I'll talk in the living room."

Curious, Marla encouraged him to stay there.

"Gretchen? Rex Alcorn. Hope you can solve an identity question for me. Do you recall anyone with the last name of Tansy living in the complex?"

He listened briefly.

"The name came up when a few of us were discussing tenants we didn't know." He listened some more. His eyes flickered. "Yeah. Right. Now I remember. At least I can place her. Any forwarding address you'd care to share?" He nodded. "Okay, thanks, Gretchen. I owe you."

Gretchen Sanstrom again. There was a story there. Marla wasn't sure she wanted to know what it was.

To her and Kitty's frustration, he returned to his slice of pizza before saying anything to them.

"I thought Gretchen Sanstrom went home with a migraine?" Marla said.

"She did, although she's feeling better. I called her personal number." He didn't offer further explanation.

Marla debated asking how he had that information and decided against pursuing it since Kitty was present.

"So?" Kitty asked. "What did you learn?"

He set down his pizza slice once again, now only a few bites left. "Arabella Tansy lived here until last spring. She burst into their office one day wanting Elliot thrown out of the building. She wouldn't say why except that he had taken advantage of her in a business deal. When they suggested she go to the police instead, she stormed from their office. She moved out two days later."

Marla and Kitty both sat forward. "Did they tell the police as much?" Marla asked.

"Tansy hadn't given them enough information to take any action other than to watch Elliot more closely. But as we've been learning, he kept a pretty low profile in the building, even though most of his marks seem to have lived here," Rex said.

"Now I remember that name," Kitty said. "Someone told me she came from one of the old families over on Summit in St. Paul. The McClellans, though she went by her father's name. The word was she was trying to make a name for herself in the world of children's books without relying on the family name. If she gave Elliot a substantial amount of money, she might have returned to the family home because she could no longer afford to live here."

"Good memory, Kitty," Rex replied. "I hadn't made the connection yet, although I investigated a robbery at the McClellan home years ago. As I recall, thieves stole some artwork while the family was away on vacation. We were able to recover most of it." He turned to Marla. "We should at least pay the family a visit. She may have returned there or they should know where else she went."

Kitty finished off her slice of pizza and sat back. "Sounds like you two have your afternoon cut out for you."

"Guess we attempt to track down Arabella Tansy," Marla said.

Rex had been staring across the room and blinked when she addressed him. "Yeah, it couldn't hurt. At least this one was furious enough to tell others. That's the first instance other than Scottie we've found of someone who's spoken up. Too bad she left before any of the residents learned her fate. She might've spared the later victims their losses."

"It sounds like the police have backed off since grilling Scottie the other day," Kitty said. "Maybe they're looking outside the building and you two can stop being amateur detectives?"

They couldn't tell her the reason the police had seemingly backed off was because they were investigating for the police. "I don't think she can breathe freely yet," Rex replied.

"We've turned up a few other suspects, but so far, even though they all had a good motive because he scammed them, too, no one sticks out as the most likely killer," Marla added.

"But that doesn't mean none of them did it," Rex was quick to add. "Just that our killer has so far been very adept at not being noticed. But then, we didn't expect whoever did the deed to step forward admitting their crime."

"In other words, you two are still on the case," Kitty said.

"That should be good news, since you won't have to worry about how to keep me entertained," Marla answered.

Kitty released a sigh. "True, although I have a long list of things I want the two of us to do. At least I know you're safe while you're with Rex."

"Good to know you no longer see me as the Big Bad Rex," Rex said, chuckling.

Kitty returned a smile only the two of them seemed to understand.

Pizza and salads finished, Marla and Rex rose in unison without realizing they were doing so.

"See ya later, sis," Marla said. "Maybe we'll have solved the case by then."

"One can only hope," Kitty said to their departing backs.

eighteen

· · ·

"Thanks for helping me deal with Kitty back there," Marla told Rex on their way to the McClellan home. "I really wanted to tell her about our deal with Goodhue, but for now I thought it best she not know we're assisting the police."

"I agree. Though I've been friends with your sister since she moved in, Kitty can be a loose cannon," Rex said. "We want to keep our investigation as low-key and quiet as possible, so the killer, if they live in the building, doesn't get advance warning."

"Why didn't you advise her about that?"

He sent her a quick glance. "You know your sister. You always wonder if she'll do exactly the opposite of what you ask of her."

"Spoken by someone who seems better acquainted with Kitty Lovejoy than you've let on thus far," she said. "Perhaps you should fill me in on how things have been between the two of you before I arrived on the scene."

He shot her a quick look, then returned immediately to the road. "We're almost there. There's not enough time to go into how things were with Kitty and me. You'll have to take a raincheck."

"I hope you're not deflecting my interest for good. Besides being curious, I think it's important for me to have some feel for your history with her if you and I are going to work well together."

He didn't reply. For now, she wouldn't push, because they needed to be in sync when they confronted Arabella Tansy and the McClellans.

The McClellan home was a Mediterranean Colonial Villa with a wrought-iron Juliet balcony streetside on the second floor. To Marla's surprise, it was not framed in front with a wrought-iron fence like several of its neighbors, and it was set somewhat closer to the street. Still, it was huge. She guessed at least six bedrooms, probably as many fireplaces.

They faced three challenges. First, they had to learn whether Arabella still lived there. Second, they needed to gain entry, since they couldn't exactly say they were the police or even that they were working for the police. And finally, even if Arabella was there and agreed to see them, would she admit to having given money to the man?

A woman about their age answered the door. Her well-coiffed hair had gone completely white. Tall and slender, she wore a dark brown cotton knit sweater and slacks. Probably a St. John.

"Hello?" Her voice carried a musical lilt.

Rex took the lead. A much more charming Rex. "Mrs. McClellan?"

"Yes?" she replied.

"My name is Rexford Alcorn, and this is ..."

"Letitia Carruthers!" the woman finished for him.

It never failed to surprise Marla how widely she was known, but in this case, she was ready to take full advantage of her celebrity, despite how much she'd tried to live it down since returning to Minnesota. "Yes, I used to play her on television," she said, extending her hand. "My real name is Marla Dane."

"Of course it is! I watched you catch killers every week for the last six years. I'm sorry those days are over."

Rather than tell the woman she was sorry, too, Marla just nodded and thanked her.

Showtime. Although they'd planned on Rex explaining their presence, she took the lead, since she had the woman's attention.

"This may sound a bit odd, but I'm still a bit of an investigator, though by no means a private eye like Letitia. I've agreed to help some of the residents at the Rambling Meadows Condominiums look into some difficulties they've experienced in the last six months. We've come to visit with your daughter, Arabella, if she's here, in hopes she can shed some light on that situation."

"Do you mean that murder?" the woman asked in the same way as if asking if Marla would prefer coffee or tea once they'd been invited in, if that would even happen.

The only way to answer her question was to be equally forthcoming. "Yes, that's right."

"I'm not sure Arabella could help you. She's been back here the last few months."

Though Marla probably could've negotiated her way through a response with the right smile, Rex took his turn. "We're aware of that, Mrs. McClellan. But she did still live there early this past year, about the same time the victim moved in. We're trying to learn as much as possible about him in order to figure out what happened."

"I doubt she would know anything about the man, but come in anyhow. She should be back in a few minutes. She drove her father over to the club. He refuses to use those rideshare people now that he can no longer drive, and since Arabella's been here, he's been leaning on her. Would you like some coffee while you wait?"

One question answered, at least.

She led them through a vast entryway over an Aubusson area rug and round table complete with an array of fall flowers. They continued toward the back of the house into the kind of room some of the old guard in California still retained but that Marla doubted ever existed in Minnesota. A sun room. Now that Marla thought about it, a sun room here in the northland made perfect sense. A huge bay window facing a well-manicured backyard occupied one entire wall. The other walls were covered in a mural of forest animals painted in muted greens, gold and cream. It must be a joy to sit here in the winter months sipping coffee or reading a book.

In other words, they had entered the world of old money. Rooms and lifestyle appeared effortless on the surface, but underneath was a vast support system financed by wealth that knew no bounds.

Her world back in LA had been something like this, although her wealth had only amassed in the last twenty years, helped in good part by her inheritance from a renowned, prolific writer. For a brief moment, a wave of regret swept over her as she recalled how things used to be and what she'd sacrificed. But that was behind her now. Continued dwelling on the past would only make her sad and defeat her current mission.

Their hostess disappeared briefly, presumably to get their coffee.

"So far, so good," Rex said under his breath.

"Let's hope Arabella is as accommodating as her mother," she whispered back to him.

Mrs. McClellan delivered the coffee and then left them alone to wait for her daughter. They'd barely taken a sip before Arabella Tansy arrived.

"I understand you're here to talk about the murder over at Rambling Meadows." She continued to stand in front of them. "You've made a trip here for nothing because I don't know anything about the man. Nothing."

Apparently they could skip preliminaries and go straight for the jugular.

"Really?" Rex replied. "We were under the impression you were seeing him socially for a bit. Long enough for him to present you with a surefire investment opportunity."

"And for you to invest thirty-five thousand dollars with him," Marla added.

Arabella's mouth firmed into a straight line, although she blinked once, most likely surprised they knew for sure she'd paid him and the exact amount. "Where did you get such an idea? Like I told you, I didn't know the man."

"When did you move back to your parents' house?" Rex asked.

"Last spring. I don't remember the exact date. Does that matter?"

Rather than answering, Marla asked a follow-up question. "Why did you come home?"

Arabella glanced around like she was looking for a place to sit, but she continued to stand. "Why are you getting so personal? It's my business why I'm here."

"Unless your decision to move out is directly related to the murder of Drake Elliot," Marla said.

"We're going around in circles. I've already told you I had nothing to do with the man."

"Yes, you have. Three times," Rex said. "But your continued denials can't negate the evidence we found in his condo that clearly lists you by name along with the date you handed over your money and the amount."

"That's what you're basing your accusation on?" she said, her tone skeptical. "The word of a dead man over mine?"

"We've already confirmed the other names, dates and amounts on what we found," Rex said. "All we have to do is check your finances to confirm you were also one of his victims."

Now she did sit down, collapsing on the love seat facing them. "You—you can't do that! You're not the police."

"That's true, Ms. Tansy, but the police do know what we're doing," Marla said.

Arabella hunched up her shoulders. "Wait, if they're aware you're here, why aren't they here with you?" she asked.

"We thought you'd be more open to helping us find his killer if it was just us. We came here to get your version of the story before checking your financial records," Rex said.

Marla breathed a sigh of relief that mentioning the police hadn't sent Rex out the door. "We realize you come from a family of means, but thirty-five thousand dollars is a lot of money for anyone. Is that why you returned to your parents' home, because you were broke?"

Arabella blew out a huff. "I thought you were just a fictional detective. The kind who solves crimes with words provided by others. Did you forget you're no longer on that show?"

Fair enough response, although an obvious ploy to put her on the defensive. Marla leaned forward, attempting to appear like she was sharing confidential information. "I returned to Minnesota never wanting to hear another word about private investigators, and then Elliot went and got himself murdered the same week I arrived. I've been looking for new projects since I left my TV show. It occurred to me that this murder case would make a great subject for some sort of television project, which is how I got involved. When I found out my new boyfriend, Rex here, was a former cop, I signed him up to help me."

Arabella stared at them both. "Do you have any idea how crazy that sounds?"

"It does, doesn't it? But that's exactly what I'm doing."

"So?" Rex pushed. "What can you tell us?"

"You don't give up, do you? Do you think I killed him?"

"Did you?" Marla asked.

"No, of course not! I haven't even admitted I knew him yet."

"I thought we were past that point," Marla said. "We're not here to accuse you or trick you into confessing. We're just trying to get as much info on the guy as possible so we can discover who took him out. Maybe he mentioned someone else when he was out with you. Or you noticed some detail about him that might help us."

"How's everything going?" Mrs. McClellan asked, slipping into the room to take a seat next to her daughter.

"Don't worry, Mom. I haven't confessed to murdering the man."

"Is that why you're here?" Arabella's mother asked Marla and Rex, her expression becoming less friendly.

"All we wanted to know was if she knew the man, and if she did, what she could tell us about him that might help us identify his killer," Marla replied.

Mrs. McClellan sat back, relaxing. "Oh. What have you told them, Bella?"

"Nothing, Mom. I won't embarrass the family further."

Mrs. McClellan gave a startled look. "Further? You haven't embarrassed us, dear. Did your father say you did?"

"No, but you and Dad had to cancel your cruise because I landed back on your doorstep."

"Not exactly. Your arrival just coincided with my decision not to put up with your father spending all his time in the casino playing poker this time. I wanted him to join me on the excursions."

"You weren't disappointed with me for losing a large chunk of my trust fund?" Arabella's voice emerged like a little girl.

"We weren't exactly happy about your poor decision, but you certainly didn't disappoint us. We're delighted you're back home with us again. This house had gotten so empty with all you kids gone."

Arabella swiped at her eyes. "Oh, Mom. I've been so worried about letting you and Dad down once again."

"Why would you think that?" Mrs. McClellan said, putting her arm around her daughter.

"My track record with men has been such a disaster. That's why I haven't told you all the details about Drake Elliot."

"I'd say there's no time like the present for sharing." Mrs. McClellan turned her attention back to Marla and Rex. "Will she get into much trouble if she tells the two of you what happened between her and this man?"

"Only if she's the one who killed him," Rex said. "And she's already told us she didn't."

The mother turned back to the daughter. "It's up to you, Bella. But I think telling us about your experience with that hustler will take a huge burden off your chest."

Tansy took a deep breath. "Okay, Mom. As long as you stay here with me."

"That was my plan, dear." She turned her gaze on Rex and eyed him closely. "We've met before, haven't we?"

"Yes, ma'am. I was part of the team that investigated a robbery on these premises years ago," Rex told her.

"That's right. A younger you without the graying hair, but we've all aged, haven't we? You weren't able to capture the culprits, but you did recover most of the artwork that was taken."

"I've always regretted not putting those crooks behind bars, but they managed to escape the country."

"Nevertheless, we appreciated getting our things back," Mrs. McClelland said. She returned her attention to her daughter. "Sorry, dear. That memory just came to me. Go on with your story."

"I never sought him out," Arabella said as she began her story. "He came up to me. I was working out in the fitness room, making myself use the elliptical machine. For some stupid reason, it's always scared me. I was standing there trying to figure out how to mount it when he entered the room. He quickly grasped my dilemma and offered a few suggestions how to approach it. Not the typical malespeak, but helpful advice. Then he moved on to the treadmill across the room and didn't hover.

"He stuck around but left me alone. When I finished, I thanked him. He dismissed how much he'd helped me and that was that. He didn't come on to me. He was simply friendly and helpful.

"I didn't see him again for another week. I was checking my box in the mailroom when he entered. He made some comment about only receiving flyers in his mail anymore, because the bulk of his correspondence he received online. I replied that I was tempted to forget about snail mail altogether, but for the fear of missing something like personal correspondence or an invitation, I hadn't given up on it entirely. That prompted a longer conversation about invites we'd both received lately, and it turned out we'd both been invited to a showing by a local artist later that week. He suggested we go together.

"He was so smooth. It came out naturally, like he'd never planned it. I was intrigued. He drove that night and afterwards suggested dinner, his treat. I stupidly refused, saying I should pay, since he'd helped me get over my fear of the elliptical, which he then refused. We wound up each paying for our own meals. There was no way I could have known at the time that he was preparing to take me for a large part of my fortune."

"How did it proceed?" Marla asked, thankful Arabella's mother had encouraged her daughter to come clean about Elliot.

"At dinner we discussed different restaurants we liked and those we'd never visited but would like to. He used that last part to follow up a few days later and suggest we check out one of that last group."

"When did he bring up investments you might consider?" Rex asked.

"He'd done his research about my family. I don't know if that was before I even met him in the fitness room, after we met at the mailboxes or after our first dinner. Looking back now, I think he targeted me from the start. He began his fishing expedition at that first dinner for which he paid by asking if I was related to the McClellans who lived on Summit. I get questions like that every so often, so it didn't alarm me. Not until he kept pressing me on the subject, asking why I was living at Rambling Meadows when I could be living the life of luxury in my parents' home."

"How did you respond?" Marla asked.

"That as much as I loved my family, I wanted to be out on my own and make my own fortune."

"Let me guess," Rex said. "He said something to indicate he might be able to help you do that. But he left it there, so if you wanted to know more, you had to ask."

She cocked her head and stared back at him. "Yes! That's exactly what happened. How did you know?"

"I spent part of my career on the bunco squad when I was in law enforcement. That's a typical pattern with scam artists. They milk their victims for personal information, and they use it as a stepping stone to promises of great wealth, but to make themselves more credible, they make their marks beg for it."

Although she had no doubt what Rex was telling Arabella was true, Marla also knew this had been the pattern they'd discovered thus far with Elliot's other victims in the building.

"Too bad I didn't come to you for advice before I committed so much of my trust fund to him," she said. "But looking back on it now, he was an expert at isolating me from anyone else's guidance."

"How did he do that, dear?" her mother asked. "You've always been so protective of your independence."

Arabella took a moment to consider her reply. "He was the one who suggested what we'd do, and he confined that to dinners out, even though I offered to cook once or twice. We didn't dine anywhere near the condos and always at a venue he suggested."

Marla recalled how Scottie had described being picked up at the front door on each of her dates with the man. "Did he insist on driving each time?" she asked.

Once again, Arabella tilted her head to the side, apparently surprised by the question. "Yes. Is that more of the pattern, Mr. Alcorn?" she asked Rex instead of Marla.

"Call me Rex. And this is Marla."

"Did he explain why he wanted to pick you up that way?" Marla asked.

"I teased him about being so secretive once, and he said it was the gentlemanly thing to do."

"No other reason?" Rex asked.

"No, why? Is that significant?"

"What was his mood when he'd pick you up? Smooth, urbane, gentlemanly?"

The young woman offered a confused look. "Yes? Wait, no, now that you ask. He didn't get out to open the door for me. I don't know why I didn't point this out to him when he told me the pickup routine was because he was a gentleman. I guess it didn't click at the time. He'd quickly glance at me as I got in, but then he'd immediately focus on leaving as fast as possible, although he kept looking in the rearview mirror. When I asked him why, he acted like I was seeing things."

"Did you notice any more of that behavior once you were on your way to your destination or the rest of the evening?" Marla asked.

"He seemed to relax once we were well beyond the condo complex, although he'd always park with the back end of the car headed in first. I kidded him once about this habit, suggesting it was for a quick getaway. He gave me the strangest look but didn't respond, and I didn't follow up. Oh, and one time this woman approached him while we were dining. She called him Derek, and she didn't appear particularly happy to see him. She asked if I was his latest 'lady friend,' and then she turned to me and said, 'He's quite the charmer. Stay alert.' Drake didn't engage with her and just dismissed her appearance as mistaken identity."

"Did her showing up alarm you?" Rex asked.

She hung her head. "By then, I was so into him, I took his word that the woman was some stranger he didn't know." She seemed to think through her own words. "In retrospect, I can't believe I'd been so blind, especially after she said, 'We need to get together soon to discuss the return of the items you borrowed from my family.'"

Marla and Rex gazed at each other. Rex followed up. "Could you describe this woman?"

Arabella closed her eyes, apparently attempting to visualize the stranger. "Not very well," she replied, shaking her head. "She was white, medium build, fortyish with brown hair. Shoulder-length, I think. I don't recall what she was wearing except she didn't seem out of place in a high-end restaurant."

"Did you ask him who she was?" Marla asked.

"Captivated as I was with him, yes, of course I asked. Her attitude was threatening. I was concerned for him. In fact, I think I was the one who suggested we finish our meal and get out of there. He didn't object, although at the time I took it to be his wanting to get to the hotel."

With Mrs. McClellan in the room, mention of the hotel momentarily cut off their questions until Mrs. McClellan noticed. "It's all right. If you need to learn more about that part of their relationship, go ahead. I'll leave, if Bella would feel more comfortable."

Marla decided for them. "That's okay, Mrs. McClellan. I don't think we need to go there unless something happened during those times that convinced you to invest your money with him?"

Arabella bit a lip. "Let's just say he picked up on my need to prove myself without my family's help. He strongly suggested I could do that by taking advantage of the investment opportunity he was offering."

"Is that when you gave him your money?" Rex asked.

"I didn't give it to him, per se. That's why it seemed like it was legit. I transferred my money through my bank to a fund on the Internet, to a link he provided. He made it seem like such a sure thing, an upscale mini mall being planned for Maple Knolls. With all the growth this town has seen in recent years, especially the level of income of new residents, it didn't seem like it could miss."

"How did you find out the fund wasn't legit?" Marla asked.

"My financial advisor called me two days later. He's the one who looks after my trust fund, although I'm old enough to access it on my own. He'd been on vacation when I transferred the money, or he would've attempted to talk me out of it."

"Did you confront Elliot?" Rex asked.

"I tried. As soon as I got off the phone with my financial

advisor, I went to his condo. He didn't answer. Nor did he respond to my calls, texts or emails. He'd gone to ground, whether he was there in the building or elsewhere."

"Did you go to the police or tell anyone else?" Marla asked, although she already knew that the young woman had gone to the building management.

"I complained to the building manager but stopped short of telling her exactly why I wanted the guy kicked out of the building. I couldn't bring myself to tell anyone how foolish I'd been. I hadn't completely cleaned out my trust fund, but the amount I'd lost was devastating. I couldn't afford to stay in there any longer, so I came home to my parents. I finally told them a few weeks later, but I begged them to keep it to themselves. My dad, well, he's still speaking to me, but he's terribly disappointed in me. Mom here has been a rock."

"But this is the first I've heard the full story," Mrs. McClellan said. "Thank you both for coming here and encouraging her to open up."

"Thank you both, as well, for talking to us," Marla replied. "This gets us closer to determining what really happened."

They left mother and daughter in each other's arms.

"I'm glad her mother was there," Marla told Rex on their way back to the condo building. "She made it easier for Arabella to share what happened." She knew from experience how debilitating secrets like Arabella's could be when not processed. "Was Elliot that charismatic?"

"He appears to have carefully picked his marks, selecting only the most vulnerable. Then he played on their fears and dreams, seemingly offering them a way to realize those dreams."

"Did we catch a break when she told us about the woman interrupting their dinner?" She asked.

"If only. We'll probably never be able to track her down," Rex replied.

"Which tells us he's pulled the same scam elsewhere in the area, although he went by the name of Derek."

"I'll text Goodhue with that item. It may help them expand their search for info about him."

Marla sat back against the seat. "We've learned a lot about the man the last two days, but I don't feel like we've come any closer to identifying his killer." She didn't bother to hide her frustration.

"Time to evaluate where we stand," Rex said. "Let's go to my condo. I have this feeling we know more than we think. We just have to analyze what we've got."

nineteen

. . .

"Here, relax with your favorite beverage," Rex said to Marla, handing her a diet soda.

"You drink this stuff, too?" she asked.

"God, no! Figuring you'd be spending more time here for a few days, I had it delivered. If the stuff helps you focus on the case, more power to it."

She saluted him with an open can. "Thanks. Your investigative powers continue to amaze me."

He shrugged but offered a crooked smile. "Just part of the service."

Did she dare take this sudden esprit de corps moment further? She dared. "While we're talking about your investigative powers, this might be a good time for you to tell me why you never became an investigator on the force."

"No."

"That was fast. You didn't even consider your answer." Just the same, she didn't regret asking.

"This isn't the time, Marla."

"Does that mean there will be a time someday?"

"Why is that important?" he asked, his tone becoming more serious.

"Because I think it's important to you, whether you admit that now or not."

"Let's talk about something else, like where we are in this investigation."

It had been a valiant effort on her part to dig deeper into his past, but clearly he wasn't ready to talk about it. To press more right now would only alienate him, and that wasn't her intent. Despite her initial reaction to the man, she was coming to like him, and she wanted to know more about him.

"Okay, where do you think we are?" she asked.

He chuckled. "Good ploy. I won't discuss my own background, so you put it back on me to summarize our progress."

"I wasn't trying to be cute. I really want your take on this situation," she replied.

He scowled briefly but appeared to shift gears. "I'd say we've almost exhausted our leads here in the condo complex, with the exception of your meeting tomorrow with Peters and tracking down Donna Walker. We've learned a lot about Elliot's technique, which included a cloak of secrecy when he picked up his victims from this building. And apparently he had good reason to be on the lookout for trouble, most likely from past victims, given the woman who approached him at the restaurant when he was with Arabella Tansy. We have a pretty good idea how much money he took from the ones we know about. We know all the particulars about his injuries, time of death, where and how his body was found, and the fact that he'd been drugged."

He stopped.

"Go on," she said.

"That's all we know for sure. We still don't know where he hid the money he scammed from his victims. Every one of his victims here at Rambling Meadows had a motive for killing him and opportunity, because any one of them could've slipped out in the middle of the night, and any one of them could've wielded the rock that slammed into his head. In other words, we're no closer to identifying who killed him than when we began." He spoke with finality.

"If we weren't so sure none of them other than Arabella Tansy complained to anyone, I would've suggested they all did it together," she said.

"The thought had occurred to me once or twice also, but the theory just doesn't hold up."

She sipped her cola, hoping the shot of caffeine would spark her ability to cut through all the info they'd collected and pinpoint their culprit. "Could this mean none of them is guilty?"

He closed his eyes, apparently considering. "Interesting theory. Doesn't get us any closer to finding the killer, but if correct, it would eliminate a lot of the extraneous details."

"How would we get from interesting theory to actual fact?" she asked.

"Solid alibis surrounding the time of death would go a long way toward marking someone off our list, but so far, not one of the persons of interest we've talked to has had one."

"Anything else?" she asked.

"Eyewitness accounts. If someone saw someone else out near the pond at the estimated time of death, we'd have something close to solid. But so far, we haven't come across anything like that."

"No one has come forth and volunteered information," she said. "But maybe we or the police haven't asked the right way or the right people."

He rose, poured himself a glass of water and sipped it thoughtfully. "I suppose we could ask Gretchen to send an email blast to all residents inquiring whether anyone saw something.

But do we really want to alert the whole building to our mission?"

"What if such a message was sent under the name of Police Chief Colman Goodhue? As part of their investigation."

"It's worth a try. I'll give him a call as soon as we're done here."

"What about the money?" she asked. "Finding it won't point to his killer, unless he had the money with him the night he was killed or if they managed to get into his condo without anyone else knowing. I just wish there was some way to recoup some or all of what our people lost."

"I'll ask Goodhue how they're coming with identifying that code we sent him," he said.

"We could also ask each of our victims for the link they were given to transfer their funds. Goodhue's forensic accounting people might be able to determine if they can be tied together and tracked to the mother lode account," she replied.

"We can try. Goodhue would probably have to get help from the St. Paul or Minnesota forensic labs, and that can take time. Their resources are always stretched."

"I should've thought of that sooner," she said as she felt for the necklace beneath her top, unable to focus on anything now but the holes in their investigation. Even her diet soda wasn't getting her mojo going.

Rex studied her to the point of making her uncomfortable. "Do I sense defeat on that face of yours?"

He was calling her on her draining commitment. Should she bluff her way through and tell him he was picking up on the wrong vibes, or should she admit she was running out of steam? "Let's just call it a momentary lapse of optimism." She waited for him to chide her for becoming a fair-weather investigator.

He surprised her. "Stand up. It's time for a hug."

She didn't let herself think about his direction but instead rose and walked into his arms. The embrace was both comfortable and comforting. He wore cologne. Light but also manly. She hadn't noticed before. And damn ... she liked it. Being in the arms of a man who wasn't on the make, besides the cologne.

Before she knew it, he released her, though he'd kept his arms around her just a tad longer than what was meant to be a friend cheering up a friend.

"Thanks, Rex. I needed that. Better than a kick in the pants," she said, attempting to lighten the mood.

"You don't deserve a kick in the pants. You've been a real trouper throughout this investigation."

She'd already learned Rex didn't say anything he didn't mean. "I never pictured myself as a real-life investigator when my stint as Letitia ended. This experience has been so much different than how she did things. She always knew what she was doing; she didn't let a few setbacks along the way deter her. But that's because her lines were provided for her. All I had to do was memorize and deliver them."

"And now you're working without a net," he said. "I can see why that would throw you. Temporarily, at least." He eyed the rest of the water remaining in his glass. "I remember when I was a kid and my older cousins tried to teach me how to water ski. I did fine holding on to the handle at the end of the rope and kept my knees bent just right as I came out of the drink. But the moment I noticed I was flying across the water with no solid ground beneath me, I let go."

His recollection took her back in time to her own efforts to pick up the sport. Her family had been guests of another family at their cabin on Christmas Lake. Their friends' kids, a few years older, were already quite adept on the water, having mastered both water skiing and slaloming. Kitty, always more of the daredevil, caught on immediately. Never one to let her little sister outdo her, Marla had willed herself to brave the water and managed to learn with great effort. But she had succeeded.

Maybe that had been Rex's intention, to remind her she had more internal strength and power than she imagined. He was much sharper than she had given him credit for.

"Did you ever get past that fear?" she asked.

He drank the rest of the water. "Well, yeah. I'm not the kind of person who lets minor challenges like fear of water skiing get to me."

"I've noticed."

"I gutted it out a few more times before I got the hang of it. But that experience has remained in the back of my mind ever since. I pull it out at times like this to remind myself I'm capable of much more than I think I am. All I have to do is persist and not let initial speed bumps get in my way."

"Thanks for sharing. You knew exactly what I needed to hear."

"Did it help?"

"Yes, I think it did. At least I'm not as down in the dumps as I was," she replied.

"Good! You're the only other person I've told this to."

Really? He wouldn't lie to her, but he could invent something when he thought it would help her past her slump. Did she even care? Even if he'd simply applied what she'd heretofore considered his very basic imagination to her situation, it meant he cared enough to help her get past her self-recrimination.

"Then I appreciate your sharing your story even more," she told him.

"Ready to get back on board our investigation bus?"

"Tell me all you know about Gordon Peters," she answered.

twenty

. . .

Since the coffee shop didn't accommodate a lot of people, Marla and Rex agreed he wouldn't go in. They didn't want his presence to prevent Gordon Peters from telling her the full story, whatever it was. Rex waited in his SUV outside in the parking lot so she could make a fast escape, if needed.

Though she attempted to arrive first, Gordon was already there waiting for her with a booth near the back of the room. She had to walk past all the other tables and booths to get there, more than likely his way of showing everyone else he'd managed to wangle a "date" with the celebrity.

"I wasn't sure you'd come," he said by way of greeting.

"I wasn't sure, either," she replied. "I debated whether you were serious about having information that might help me learn more about the Elliot murder."

"Quite serious, my dear," he said. "I'll tell you what I know just as soon as I get you a cup of coffee and a sweet roll."

"Just coffee for me. Black. I don't eat much in the morning."

His left brow rose. "That's not healthy."

"Nor are most sweet rolls," she returned.

He didn't argue but instead went to the counter to place the order. A minute later, he was back with two mugs. "Here you go. Black, like you requested."

Since her beverage was still hotter than she wanted to sample, she sat back and offered an expectant look.

"Such impatience," he said. "I thought you movie stars sat around several hours a day waiting for your few minutes of filming."

"More recently, I appeared in a television drama, not films," she corrected. "TV is faster-paced." She let that sink in while she waited for him to get to the point.

Finally, after consuming over half the contents of his mug, he set it down. By now, most of the patrons who had ogled her when she arrived had taken off. Other than the coffee shop staff, they were alone. Gordon had delayed saying anything she wanted to hear until he knew they'd have relative privacy.

"Elliot was scum," he began.

"So I've been learning. Why does he rate that opinion from you?"

"He almost ruined the life of a young woman I know. My niece, Noelle Donnelly. She lived at Rambling Meadows with me until recently, until she barely escaped certain imprisonment and humiliation at the hands of that guy."

Marla guessed. "She was a victim of his romantic charms?"

He sucked in his lips and shook his head violently. "Hook, line but not sinker. She was living with me because her parents moved to the north country and she didn't want to walk away from her chance of advancement at the marketing company she worked for downtown as an accountant. Soon after she moved in, the HOA board got wind of her skills and persuaded her to fill out the unexpired term of its former treasurer. Once Elliot discovered her role, he moved in on her, wining and dining her every few days to the point she couldn't think straight.

"He was always on her mind. 'Drake said this and Drake did

that.' At first, I was happy for her. She'd been pretty down when she first moved in. Missed her parents. Had dated some but didn't have much experience with men. I didn't really worry about her seeing Elliot at first because I thought he'd get bored with a young woman with very little experience. But I was wrong. I misjudged his intentions. Before I knew what was happening, he'd convinced her to invest in a land scheme. A development supposedly going in south of town.

"Problem was, she didn't have ten thousand dollars to invest. But that didn't bother him. 'Borrow it from the HOA fund,' he told her. 'You'll have doubled your money before they miss it.' She woulda done exactly that, except she couldn't get the link to the HOA fund to work and had to ask me how to do it. She couched her problem in terms that had nothing to do with 'borrowing' from the fund, but she finally broke down when I continued to press her and told me about the sure-fire investment Elliot had encouraged her to make."

The niece was the Donnelly name on Elliot's list of his takings. "You stopped her?" Marla asked.

"Then. Since she'd only attempted to embezzle the money, no harm, no foul, although I convinced her she had to resign from her post. Our relationship went downhill after that. Guess she was embarrassed that I'd caught her. She moved out a month later and joined her parents up north. All I hear about her now is through her parents, who are totally ignorant of what she'd almost done."

"Has she been back since?" Rex asked.

"Not likely. Shortly after she joined them, she fell and broke her leg. She's been in a wheelchair since."

So much for that lead.

"Gordon, you could've told me all this other night," she said, unable to dismiss the feeling she'd been duped.

"Maybe," he responded, looking sheepish.

"Not maybe. You could've told me all that in six sentences."

"Perhaps, but ..."

"But then you wouldn't have been able to show me off to your friends."

He didn't answer. He had the cheek to appear embarrassed as his neck grew pink.

"It's okay, Gordon. I'm used to people leveraging my celebrity to impress others."

He jerked. "Oh, my. Is that how this little coffee date came across? I'm sorry. I apologize." He paused. "You're right. I was trying to impress the guys but not with your celebrity. In fact, I almost forgot about that. But I was trying to impress them with you. You're a beautiful woman, Marla. I'm sure you know that. You may have been a terrific actress on that show of yours, but you have to admit, your looks got you in the door in the first place."

She opened her mouth to contradict him but stopped. She wasn't unaware of the power of her appearance. Gordon Peters had simply acted like a man, a man who used a woman's desire for information to get closer to her. At least he'd been honest with her and hadn't denied her accusation.

"Thanks for the compliment," she said. "Maybe my looks got me noticed in the early days of my stage career, but it was my professional reputation that got me the job portraying Letitia Carruthers."

He held up a hand. "Sorry. Thought at our age, reference to your looks would be more appreciated."

She ignored his none-too-swift reference to her age. "Thanks for sharing your story about your niece. I hope she's back on her feet soon." She rose. "I think I've had enough coffee for now."

She marched out of the coffee shop and climbed into Rex's SUV to bring him up to date. "We can take one more name off the list," she said, and brought him up to speed about Noelle Donnelly.

His shoulders sagged. "Damn! I was hoping Peters was our killer."

"You don't particularly care for the man?"

"He cheats at golf."

"You play golf?" She couldn't keep her disbelief out of her voice.

"On occasion. Why so surprised?"

Had she unintentionally insulted him? "I guess I pegged you as more of a bowler or on a baseball team."

He rubbed his jaw. "At least you picture me as a team player. Am I not suave enough for golf?"

"Suave?" She couldn't help but laugh. "I haven't heard that word in years. Golfers need a lot of patience, waiting for others to take their shots and then lining up their own shots. I see you more as a man of action."

He grinned, something he didn't do often. "Nice save. You didn't know me when I was on the force. Stakeouts and examining multitudes of evidence took a lot of patience."

"My comment was meant as an observation, not an insult, Rex."

"Yeah? Okay. Anyway, Peters apparently is innocent, at least about Elliot's death. Which leaves us with only one more person to interview."

"Donna Walker. Have you met her?"

He shook his head. "No, this one has eluded my attempt to meet everyone in the building."

"Losing your touch?"

He pulled his head back. "Of course not! It happens. It's not like I'm the official greeter. Or a busybody, like you may suspect. And I've more or less been out of commission the last few days while I've been on the case with you."

"You didn't have to ..."

"Oh, yes, I did," he inserted. "Goodhue knew exactly what button to push when he pulled me into your investigation."

"The same button you won't discuss with me?"

"Not today."

"Then I guess it's time to track down Donna Walker." If this lead went nowhere, it was back to the drawing board.

twenty-one

. . .

As with Gordon Peters, they decided Marla would approach Donna Walker alone, until she got in the door. Two of them at her door might work against them.

As it turned out, their strategy wasn't necessary. Donna Walker wasn't home. At least she didn't answer the door.

Rex checked the Rambling Meadows directory on his phone. "Let's try the old-fashioned way and phone her."

"You have the entire Rambling Meadows directory on your phone?" she asked.

"Saves time. Like now."

Rather than call while standing in front of Donna Walker's door, which would've been tacky, they headed down the hall to the community room. For once it was open, so they could call her in private.

Marla introduced herself over voicemail and gave a thumbnail description of why she needed to see Walker. "What are the chances she'll get back to me?" she asked.

"Depends on whether she recognizes your name and, if she does, whether it's worth it to her to meet you in person."

She shook her head. "I came here to escape my life in LA

and forget about my celebrity. Instead, what have I done almost since my first day here? Used it to gain access to information."

"Too late to go back or cry over spilled milk," he returned. No sympathy there.

She moved on. "Now that we've talked to almost everyone on our list, I keep wondering what we've missed. If our killer has been in this group, how can we get the truth from them?"

"Was that a rhetorical question?"

"It started out that way, but I'd really like to know," she replied. "Letitia typically interviewed suspects once, and then some off-the-wall piece of evidence occurred to her so she could zero in on the offender. Usually around the fifty-minute mark. When will we reach our fifty minutes?"

He sank into one of the room's comfy easy chairs. "I told you going into this exercise, it wouldn't be like you were back in front of a TV camera."

"I'm well aware of that. I just hoped that at this point in our partnership you'd have some pithy advice to keep me believing we can do this."

"I didn't realize providing *pithy* advice was in my job description," he replied.

She released a sigh. "It isn't. I was just trolling for a pick-me-up."

"Hmm. Too early for a drink. Want to go run a mile with me?"

"Are you serious?" She could never tell when this man was pulling her leg.

"Not really. Already did that this morning at six. But if you think it would help, I'll accompany you."

She chuckled. "I should've known. Thanks for the offer, but I'll pass this time."

He sat back and lifted one knee over the other. "Good. Not

sure I would've been up to the task anyhow, although I would've faked it if you'd been interested."

"Aren't you lucky running isn't high on my list of things I like to do?" she joked.

"I'll keep that in mind in the future. But since you seem to need some kind of encouragement, here are my thoughts. First, like I've already said, talking to persons of interest once is just a beginning. We have to go back at least one more time. Maybe more. Interrogation isn't exactly a science, but it can be an art. Sometimes there are no results. But sometimes, a person will start to add more details or embellish what they've already told you just because they're tired of hearing their own voice or they want to get you off their back. Those are the times you wait for and listen for, and if they occur, you pounce. They may take you nowhere, but they may give you just enough leverage to pry the case open."

"You've told me some of this before, but thanks for going back over it. Your words come at just the right time."

"Good. I'm sharing the so-called *wisdom* it took me years on the job to truly understand."

She was touched. The doubting, surly skeptic who let her into Kitty's condo just days ago had turned into a caring partner. Saying thanks didn't seem to be enough.

"There's more, if you want to hear it," he said.

"Of course. What else?"

"We have to get more creative when it comes to finding evidence. The forensics team culled all it could find at the murder scene, which wasn't much. We should start there, with their notes. See if any new questions emerge or if something they found suggests a new direction. Beyond that, we should truly brainstorm what kinds of behavior, statements or whatever could lead us to the killer."

"You make it sound like a parlor game," she said, her interest level rising from its low a few minutes ago.

"It's not like it's fun, but if it gets us back on a positive track, it's worth considering."

Her phone rang at that point. "Ms. Dane? This is Donna Walker. Sorry I missed you earlier. I'm back, but just for a little while, so why don't we meet now? Perhaps in the lobby? My cleaning lady is here right now."

"How about the community room instead?" Their voices would reverberate all over the place in the small lobby reception area.

"Okay. I'll see you shortly."

"Just so you know, I'll have a friend with me."

"Oh? Okay."

She hung up and turned to Rex. "Ready, *friend?*"

IF MARLA HAD BEEN GIVEN a hundred chances to guess the description of Donna Walker, she still would have failed. "Nondescript" might have been her best try. Walker's appearance was the epitome of average. Height somewhere around five foot five. Weight somewhere between one twenty and one thirty. Eye color dirty blue tinged with brown. Hair color somewhere in the brown family; it appeared to be between color treatments.

"You really are the famous television star," Walker said by way of greeting when she joined them in the community room. "I'd heard rumors of your temporarily living in the complex but didn't know whether to believe them."

"My sister, Kitty Lovejoy, is a resident here. I needed a break from my life in LA and took her up on her offer for me to visit," Marla answered.

"You said you're developing a new project for TV and wanted

my input," Walker said. "I can't imagine why, but I was curious enough to hold off leaving for my appointment to talk to you." She turned to Rex. "Are you her manager or agent or whatever you entertainment folks are called?"

"No, ma'am, I'm not connected with the industry. Like she told you, I'm a friend who's serving as her second set of eyes and ears."

"You look familiar."

Charming Rex was back. "I live in the building, too." He offered a smile. Had he ever smiled at her like that?

Walker smiled back. "Ah, yes. I must have seen you in passing, although I don't get out much. I work at home."

Time to get to the point. "The TV project I'm considering would be a limited series about the Drake Elliot murder. I've been told you knew him. Is that correct?"

Walker, who'd remained standing, took a step back. A small one but still a step. Her forehead wrinkled. "Where did you hear that?"

Marla didn't answer her directly. "That doesn't matter. If that's the case, I'd like to get your read on him."

"I haven't even said I knew him."

"I heard wrong?" Marla returned with mock innocence. The woman hadn't lied yet, but she was holding back. Simply being cautious or did she not want to admit she had known him? And if the latter, why?

"Perhaps it would jog your memory if we told you we found evidence in his condo that included your name," Rex told her, cutting to the chase.

Walker's eyes widened ever so slightly. "How would that prove I knew him?"

"Okay," Marla followed up, "how about we found texts and emails from him to you and vice versa."

Walker's mouth remained firmly shut.

"Why are you denying you knew him?" Marla asked. "There's no shame in admitting he played you the same way he did others we've talked to."

Walker pounced on that statement. "You've talked to others?"

Marla kept her tone even, refusing to let the other woman put her on the defensive. "Yes. As I told you, I'm doing a sort of mini-investigation to unearth the facts of the case. Elliot apparently preyed on several women in this complex, getting them to invest substantial sums of money in fake accounts. Money that made its way to his personal accounts."

"Have you located those?" Walker asked too quickly for someone who still hadn't admitted she'd known the dead man.

"Why would you be interested, Ms. Walker, if you didn't know him?" Rex asked.

"Curious, that's all. I'm sorry those women got taken." She glanced at her watch. "Look, I agreed to this get-together because I wanted to meet you, Ms. Dane, but I need to be on my way to my appointment. I'm already five minutes behind schedule." She headed for the door.

Desperate to gain some bit of information from the woman, Marla drew on one of Letitia's tactics. "Wait!" she called to Walker, who stopped just short of the exit. "What if I told you we've spoken to an eyewitness to one of your dates?"

"Really?" Walker studied her. "Supposing I call your bluff. Who purportedly saw me with him? When and where?"

So much for borrowing one of Letitia's tactics. People always believed the fictional PI when she invented evidence. Marla stalled, trying to decide how to respond.

"We're not at liberty to divulge that information," Rex, now in cop mode, answered for her.

Walker nodded. "That's what I thought." She pivoted and was out the door before either Marla or Rex could respond.

They exchanged looks with each other. Had they gained anything from that brief exchange?

"Interesting," Rex said at length.

"You seem to say that word whenever you're trying to make sense of an otherwise senseless situation."

He pulled at his collar. "I didn't realize I'd become so transparent. I'll have to watch that habit."

"Please don't. It's one of the few ways I can attempt to read you," she replied.

He grimaced. "At the moment, you should've been reading Donna Walker. What was your takeaway?"

"My immediate reaction to her hasty departure was that we'd gained nothing. But on second thought, her not admitting anything told us quite a lot."

He gave her the same smile he'd given Walker when he met her. "You're learning. Tell me what you made of it."

She was so anxious to share her sudden insight, she didn't wonder if he was already there or just faking. "If she really never met him, let alone gone out with him, she would've said so directly. But instead, she challenged us as to how we supposedly knew. She definitely knew him, but I suspect, unless he didn't record his take from her, which I seriously doubt, she didn't give him any money."

Rex had nodded his head throughout her statements. "And if she didn't, why wasn't she crowing about it instead of denying she'd had anything to do with him?" he asked.

"If she didn't give him any money, why not? What kept her from falling for his line unlike the others?"

Rex held up a hand. "Great questions, but don't get too carried away with them until we know a few more things about her."

"Like what?"

"Like, who is she? Do we know anything at all about the woman?" he asked.

"If we check with Gretchen Sanstrom, we should be able to get the specific date of her arrival."

"Good idea," Rex replied.

"Do you think Sanstrom would share any of the due diligence she must've done on Walker to approve her moving in?"

"All we can do is ask."

"Did she even buy the condo, or was she renting?" Marla asked. "Do we even know if the others we've questioned own or are renting?"

"That fact probably doesn't matter as much with them," he replied. "In all of those cases, even with Gordon Peters, they are known quantities. They've all lived here at least a year. Donna Walker is the only recent resident."

She rose and was about to stand where Walker had just planted herself when Rex called out. "Stop! Don't touch anything over there."

"What? You mean this chair?" Then his sudden interest in her location hit her. "She put her hand on the back of this chair as she stood here talking to us. Maybe she left fingerprints."

"Stay put while I go to my condo. I'll be right back. If anyone else comes into the room, don't let them near the chair, but don't give anything away."

Charming Rex was now gone. He'd been replaced with Man-of-Action Rex. She should resent his abrupt exit but didn't. She was getting accustomed to his MO, and she found it sexy. *Hold up, Marla. Don't get carried away.*

He was back within five minutes. "Had to do some rooting around in my closet, but I finally found this tucked away behind some other mementos from the old job." He opened a slim black leather case. "Although the forensics team had the official fingerprint paraphernalia, seasoned cops purchased their own mini kits. Even though I tried to put that life behind me, I kept a few things that might come in handy someday."

"And that day has arrived," she said.

"If I remember how to do this properly. I should probably contact Goodhue and have him get a team out here that knows what they're doing. But I'd prefer we continue to keep our actions low-key and wait until we absolutely have to bring in Goodhue and his people."

"Do it. If we later find we need to get her prints officially, Goodhue can always serve a warrant to go into her place."

"Good point," he replied.

He poured some powder over the section of the chair back where Walker had rested her hand, then carefully dusted the residue away so he could collect the prints. "I'll have Goodhue send someone over here to pick this up."

"He won't be upset that you proceeded without his people?"

"Thanks to your backup plan, he should be okay with my reasoning, especially if I explain we're concerned she could take off at any time since we've talked to her."

"Now who's getting carried away?" she asked. "You're acting like she's our killer."

"I'm not there yet. But I got bad vibes hearing all the road-blocks she threw at us. She didn't even want to meet at her condo. In fact ... let's go."

He quickly packed up his kit and secured the results, then headed for the door, Marla in his wake.

No one answered the door at Walker's condo. They knocked three different times and got no response each time.

"That doesn't mean she didn't have a cleaning person in there earlier," Marla said. "They could've left already."

"Let's go to the manager's office," he replied.

Iris Cadell greeted them. "Are you two still snooping around the Elliot murder?"

Marla let Rex handle Cadell. "Surely you're anxious to relieve the condo complex of any responsibility relating to the man's death?" Rex said. "We're getting close, but we need some information from you that hopefully will get us closer to discovering what happened."

Mr. Charming had returned. This metamorphosis must be killing Rex. How much Nice Guy could he handle?

Cadell took another few seconds to appear to think through his words, but in the end, she relented. "What do you want to know?"

Rex turned it over to Marla.

"Is Donna Walker renting, or does she own the condo she's in?"

"Renting."

"When did she sign the lease, and when did she move in?" Marla continued.

Cadell checked her computer. "The lease was signed two days before she moved in, which was August 3."

Now Rex got involved again. "Who owns the condo?"

Cadell gave them the name of Porter Atwood, who lived in Tampa, Florida. She also provided Atwood's contact information.

"Do you know if Ms. Walker uses a cleaning service?" Rex asked. "I have to register the name and contact information of mine so they can get into the building."

Cadell went back to her computer. "I don't have any notations about a cleaning service, which doesn't mean she doesn't use one. Sometimes those details slip by."

"She said she works from home," Marla said. "Do you have any details you can share about her place of employment?"

"Wentworth Enterprises, according to her application," Cadell said.

Rex telegraphed to Marla that he was finished if she was. They thanked Cadell and left.

"You said before we should be collecting more evidence," Marla said on their way to his condo. "I'd say we now have exactly that for the time being."

twenty-two

. . .

Though it was getting close to noon, neither Marla nor Rex was hungry for lunch. Not until they'd followed up on what they'd learned from Iris Cadell.

First up, contact Porter Atwood. Rex did the honors and put the conversation on speaker.

"Yes, I rented my condo in Maple Knolls to a woman named Donna Walker," Atwood answered after Rex had provided a brief explanation of why he was calling. "Has something happened to her or to my condo?"

"Nothing has happened to your condo, but there's been an incident here on the condominium grounds," Rex said. "I'm a former police officer who lives in the building, and I'm working with the police to learn more about it. A man was killed. Ms. Walker may or may not have known him."

"Sorry, can't help you there. I've never met the woman. She contacted me through my rental agent, who checked out her credentials."

"Perhaps I should speak with the rental agent," Rex replied. "Could you tell me who to contact?"

Atwood parted with that information.

"I have another question before you hang up," Rex said.

"Okay?"

"Have you ever lived in your condo here in Maple Knolls?"

"I did until last year. Decided I couldn't take another winter up north and bought a place here in Florida. Ms. Walker was the first renter. I didn't want to handle the details long-distance, so I signed on with this rental agent." He paused but didn't end the call. "Look, if there's something hinky going on with her, I need to know."

"Of course, although at the moment she appears to be legitimate and in the clear."

Rex thanked Atwood and signed off.

"We need to call this rental agent, Sean McCoy at McCoy Rental Management," he told Marla.

She volunteered to call him. "Donna Walker, you say?" McCoy replied after she'd gone through an explanation close to what Rex had used with Atwood. "I remember her because she wanted to pay her rent in cash, although she had a credit card. And she was quite adamant that the condo had to be in that particular building."

"Did you ever meet her?" Marla asked.

"Not that I recall. She lived out of state at the time she arranged to rent the condo."

She waited while he pulled up Walker's prior address on his computer.

"Anything else you can recall about her?"

"She asked about building security. I didn't think anything of it at the time, because she appeared to be a single woman who'd be living alone. Her main concern was that there was at least one other exit from the building besides the front entrance and the underground garage. When I told her there was, she wanted to know if someone leaving the building from that door could be seen from anywhere else in the building. At the time, I chalked it up to a need for privacy, but now that I think about it, it does seem a bit over the top, doesn't it?"

Marla didn't answer directly. "Is that a typical question you receive from clients?" she asked instead.

"Well, no. Can't think that it's ever come up before, now that you ask. Not even with the few high-profile folks I've rented to."

She had no idea why someone would ask such a question. "Did she say why she asked?"

"Let me think. She said something, if I can just recall. Oh, right. She didn't come right out and say it, but she intimated that she'd be entertaining late at night and she preferred her guest, or was it guests, I can't remember which, depart without the rest of the world knowing."

"That didn't send up any red flags with you?" Marla asked.

"No. I hear stranger things from other clients. I've learned not to pay too much attention to them, unless they signal potential trouble. Her comment flew under the radar."

She asked a few more questions, but McCoy wasn't much more help. He'd only talked to Donna Walker once. Marla thanked him and hung up.

She recounted to Rex what she'd learned from McCoy.

"Her only forms of ID were a credit card and an old address?" he asked when she finished. "No bank?"

"No. She told him she'd pay by cash, which she'd give the building manager each month."

He rubbed the back of his neck, taking in what she'd told him. "A real woman of mystery, with the exception of the credit card and a former address. My guess is they're bogus. Did McCoy say whether he'd checked them out?"

"He hedged when I asked how he verified her info. If he'd followed through, he would've said so immediately."

"Goodhue can verify both," he said as he texted the man.

"Where does that leave us while we wait for him to look into everything we've forwarded to him?"

"We still have to check out that company she said she works for," he replied, pulling up his phone. "Hello, I'm calling to verify the employment of Donna Walker," he told the person who answered, putting her on speaker.

"Who is calling and why do you need it?" the person on the other end of the line asked.

"I'm a former police officer working with the Maple Knolls Police Department on a homicide case. Ms. Walker is a person of interest."

"We can't help you," the person replied. "We have no record of someone by that name working for us."

"Perhaps she goes by a different first name with you folks?"

"No. No Donna. No Walker."

"How 'bout I speak to someone in your human resources department?" he said.

"I am HR. In fact, I'm the CEO and the entire workforce."

Rex shrugged when he got off the phone. "Wherever Walker is getting her money, it's not coming from Wentworth Enterprises. That's not to say there's something fishy about her finances. They're just somewhat unorthodox."

"We've checked out or have Goodhue and company checking out everything she told us," Marla said. "What do we do while we wait to hear from him?"

"Hungry?"

"Now that you mention it. Investigating murders takes a lot out of you."

"I've got some frozen dinners in my freezer, if you're interested," he said.

"Uh, thanks, but frozen dinners have never been high on my list of favorite foods."

"I didn't mean the commercial kind. These are meals I've been given by others in the building."

"Given?" she asked, narrowing her eyes. The unexpected twists in this man's life just kept rolling in.

"Yeah. Seems like someone's always stopping by to make sure I'm eating. Some women just can't accept the idea that a single male can fend for himself when it comes to meals."

Without replying, she walked over to his refrigerator and opened not the freezer door to admire his cache but the main door. As she suspected, the shelves held four bottles of beer, one orange, half a grilled cheese sandwich on a small plate and a candy bar. She opened the door wider for him to see. "Really? Where would they have gotten that idea?"

"I eat out a lot. So what?"

"How would your admirers know?" She didn't think he'd answer, but for reasons she couldn't explain even to herself, she wanted to make him uncomfortable.

"Okay, so we won't select a frozen dinner. Want to order out? I've got ten food places on speed dial. Except I'm not ready for another pizza."

She closed the refrigerator door and opened the freezer door. "Rex, I was kidding. I'm not at all surprised you have so many people concerned about your eating habits. You seem to have that effect on others, women and men, whether you're going for it or not." She took a few seconds to gaze at the contents. "How does beef and macaroni sound? It must have been baked already, so all we have to do is stick it in the microwave a few minutes."

She handed it over to him, and he did the honors with the microwave.

"I didn't ask for any of them," he told her as they waited for their meal to warm. "Nor did I even hint."

"I can believe that. I've seen how others react to you. I think most of the residents here at the complex are in awe of the big, tough former cop. They want to be on your team. They do things like bring you meals, since cooking doesn't seem to be your forte. One of the few things."

"Let's go back over what we've learned from those we've interviewed other than Donna Walker," Rex said as he got out plates and utensils.

They took turns reciting everything they'd learned from Scottie, Kaitlin, Rita, Arabella and Gordon.

When the timer on the microwave dinged, they spent the next twenty minutes consuming their meal. Marla finished first. "That was quite tasty. Be sure to thank 'whoever' for her efforts."

Rex took their plates and utensils and stuck them in the dishwasher. "I run this about every three days, since I don't tend to dirty many dishes." He returned to the kitchen table, where she was seated, and sat again. "Now that we've gone back over our interviews, any new thoughts occur to you?"

"Not really, other than it's become more and more clear to me what a despicable person he was. I can't condone anyone for murdering another human, but in his case, I can understand why someone was driven to it. What about you?" she asked Rex.

"During my years on the force, I unfortunately saw my share of 'despicable' people and victims too embarrassed to report their losses to the police."

"Without your no-nonsense approach to this case, I would've quit by now as we've learned more and more about that guy," she said.

"Listen to you being my cheerleader. I can use the points for serving you nothing more than a frozen dinner."

"A frozen dinner prepared by another woman, no less," she replied, laughing.

He cocked his head to the side. "You gonna hold that against me the rest of our lives?"

"How 'bout the rest of the day? I finally found something that gets under your skin. I want to make the most of it."

"And that's important to you? More important than solving this case?" he said in a serious tone.

She'd only been teasing him in an attempt to lighten the mood. But he wasn't ready to go there. "Those are two different things, Alcorn. Of course, I want to solve this case. Soon, too. It's starting to get to me. But when I agreed to team up with you, I never figured dealing with an ex-cop who seemed to rule the nest would be such a challenge."

He stared at her with laser focus. "Challenge? Nest? Where's this coming from? Have I done something to offend you?"

He didn't appear to accept her joking tone. She had to come clean as best she could. "No, not exactly. When I first arrived, you acted put out to have to come and let me into Kitty's place."

"For which I thought I apologized, even that night. You pulled me away from a Twins game. One doesn't give up his Twins Games late in the season unless it's absolutely necessary. That's why I was so grumpy. Plus, I was pissed once again at your sister that she could be so thoughtless and not be there to greet you."

"You're right. You did apologize. I guess I was just so overwhelmed with Kitty being gone and leaving no message why she was gone, your apology got buried. Then, within a few days, you were pulled back into my orbit again, this time by Goodhue to help me on this case. I had no idea what he'd done until he'd done it. But I felt like you blamed me."

He scratched his chin. "Thought I explained all that at the time. Yeah, I guess I wasn't happy to be called in on this case, but that had little to do with you. More to do with my continuing bad blood with Goodhue."

"And events that occurred years ago," she said. "Events you refuse to discuss with me."

Rex blew out a breath, then stared at his hands several seconds. "Okay. We've come this far together on this case. I guess I trust you enough to share a headline version of what happened."

She wasn't expecting him to cave so soon, but fine. She wanted to know. She clasped her hands together and waited.

He stared across the room, as if seeking the right words. "From the first day I joined the force, my goal was to be a homicide detective. I was well aware I had to earn that right, and I was prepared to do so. I listened to and learned from the senior officers. My test scores and evaluations were exemplary. As luck would have it, though, Colman Goodhue wanted the same thing, and openings for detectives on the homicide squad didn't come often. We were rivals from the first day we met, and it didn't take long for everyone to know about it and take advantage of it."

He paused. Did he want her to ask more questions? She complied. "How did they do that?"

"In a lot of little ways, but mainly whenever there was a dirty job to be done and none of them wanted to do it, they dangled it in front of us both and enjoyed the show, watching us vie to get the honor. We went out of our way attempting to one-up each other more than once, and sometimes that backfired. One or both of us emerged looking foolish and ridiculous.

"In the beginning, these competitions were limited to non-life-threatening situations. Our so-called 'pals' on the force were savvy enough to avoid putting our lives on the line. But when the retirement of one of the senior detectives was imminent, we got more daring. I don't want to get into the details, but suffice it to say, we put ourselves in a situation perilous to both of us. We were both nearly killed, and Goodhue wound up saving my life."

"Which he apparently never lets you forget," Marla said.

"There's that, but the outcome of that situation was that we both blew our chances to become homicide detectives. At least at that time, while our current superior was still in his job. My disappointment in myself permeated my marriage. I was divorced within a few years. Goodhue also got divorced, although he's remarried since. That's the woman in your book club. Patty."

She didn't know how to react. He'd told her most of what she'd been wanting to hear, but it didn't jibe with the man she'd been working with. He'd described a man so intent on winning, he'd lost his better judgment. Rex wasn't like that. Was he?

She was so caught up in her own thoughts, for several beats she didn't notice him studying her.

"Well? No comments?" he asked at last.

"I don't know what to say, Rex, other than thank you for feeling you could tell me what happened back then in your police career."

"Yeah, well, I could say you browbeat me into revealing my past, but that's not true. I decided I wanted to tell you. At least some of it. The details don't matter anymore."

One other question lingered in her mind. He'd already shared so much. But if she didn't ask now, she might not ever find out. "Now that I have some idea why you said yes to Good-hue's request, how did you feel about pairing up with me?" Did she really want to hear what he'd say?

"Feel? By now you should know I don't talk about my feel-ings," he replied.

"You still have them, though. I know you weren't crazy to be working with me when we first started, but ..."

"But have I changed my mind? You really want to know? What if I said no? Could you deal with the letdown?"

"What makes you think I'd be let down?" she replied. Of course she'd be, but why tell him?

"You wouldn't be you if you weren't. You care what people think of you. That's probably what got you into acting."

"So?" She was pushing. More than she should. But he was right. She cared.

"Okay, yeah, I wasn't pleased to get stuck with you as part of repaying the debt I owed Goodhue. But I played good soldier and went along with the plan. I fully intended to be doing all the heavy lifting in our investigation. But no way was I about to pamper the Hollywood Princess."

"Is that how you thought of me?"

"At first. But as it turned out, you haven't been that way at all. Don't let this go to your head, but you've been a pretty good partner."

They stared at each other for several beats. He'd said a lot. Probably more than he intended to say. She didn't know what to say next. She didn't want to break the spell.

She didn't have to worry about a follow-up because his phone rang.

twenty-three

· · ·

The caller was Goodhue.

"Okay if I put you on speaker?" Rex asked. "I'm in my kitchen with Marla. We've been rehashing everything we've learned from our interviews. Have you got any new info for us?"

"Sure, put me on speaker. You both should hear this at the same time. First item, the two of you have done a bang-up job gleaning a lot of background information about our victim. That list naming his victims and the dates and amounts of their investments was a huge help."

"What about the code? Have you been able to track it down?" Rex asked.

"Not yet, although we're making progress. We think it will lead to a private bank account somewhere. None we've been able to locate in Minnesota, anyhow. But the guy who's been working on it, one of the forensic accounting guys from the state, thinks those first few numbers might relate to a system in the Caribbean. Not one of the usual suspects. Something smaller."

"Is the same person reviewing those links I sent you, the ones his victims used to transfer their funds?"

"Nah. I didn't want to complicate the state guy's job. I know a guy with the St. Paul PD who loves to track down that kind of detail. Whoever set up the system for Elliot knew their way around computers. It's taking the St. Paul guy longer than he first thought would be the case. Just be patient. If it's the yellow brick road to the money, that will be good, but it won't help us find the murderer," Goodhue said.

"Speaking of which, what, if anything, have you learned about Donna Walker?" Rex asked.

"Not much yet. The fingerprints you sent us weren't as clear as we'd like. Even if we can isolate something and find a match in the system, a defense attorney could have a field day establishing chain of custody."

"Sorry. I did my best to keep the process legit. Anyway, we don't need them so much to prove guilt as to identify the woman. She wasn't the most forthcoming with details about her life."

"I'm already beginning to see that," Goodhue replied. "The only Donna Walker we've been able to find died a year ago. My guess is that your Donna Walker borrowed the name."

"I had a feeling that was the case. It tells us she's been lying about who she is. And that's huge."

"Still, it doesn't necessarily tie her to the murder."

Rex exchanged a look with Marla. He'd apparently been hoping to hear more. "True, but her so-called employer has never heard of her. How about the credit card? Were you able to learn anything from that?"

"Still checking on that one. Apparently credit card companies have gotten very close with their data these days. Had to send them something official. Since it's the weekend, may not hear back until Monday at the earliest."

"Anything else?" Rex asked.

"Hold on. I'm checking my list." He went off the line a few beats. "Ah, yes. The former address she gave the rental agent?

Bogus. There is a Carbondale, Illinois, but no Laughton Avenue and thus no 445 Laughton Avenue. That came directly from the Carbondale PD. Add that one to your list of negatives about the woman."

"A fast-growing list," Rex observed. "But nothing so far links her to Elliot."

"Wait!" Marla said. "What about that newspaper clipping we found in Elliot's condo?"

Rex thunked his head. "I got so excited about the list of names and that code, I forgot about the clipping. I'll take a photo of it and send it to you immediately. It doesn't necessarily tie the woman to his death, but other than those other two items, it was the only other personal item we found in his condo."

"I'll get on it as soon as I receive it," Goodhue replied. "Patty wanted to go to some art gallery reception. It'll give me an excuse to skip it. When she gets upset, I'll tell her I just received it from her favorite TV detective."

Marla didn't get a chance to reply because Goodhue ended the call.

"Great. Now Patty will blame me for ruining her night," she said.

"If I know Goodhue, he'll assign one of his underlings to the clipping and will still go with Patty. But not until he tells her of the sacrifice he made to be on her arm."

She chuckled. "I thought you said you no longer saw him socially?"

"I don't. But he hasn't changed that much since the old days. He wasn't a bad police officer, but he wasn't above taking advantage of a situation when it worked to his benefit."

"We all do that once in a while" she said.

"Let's just say he refined taking advantage to a fine art."

"So? We got just enough confirmation from our pal the

police chief to not dismiss Donna Walker as a suspect but not enough to quiz her again," she said.

"That's about the size of it."

"And?"

"Now we wait, unless there's anything more you can think of for us to do?"

"I'm too hyped to just relax. How about we go back over the police notes?"

He raised a brow. "Aren't you the glutton for punishment?"

"Now that we've got a better feel for the man and his exploits, maybe something will grab our attention."

"Has anyone ever told you how persistent you are, Marla Dane?"

"I didn't survive twenty years in Hollywood without developing a tough exterior and pushing for my better interests, at least until this past year."

He leaned his elbows on the counter. "If ever there was a lead-in. Ready to tell me what happened out there to bring you here?" he asked. "I revealed my past to you. Now it's your turn."

It probably was, but things were going relatively well with her new partner. Was she ready to risk jeopardizing whatever relationship they were developing? "You just don't want to go back over those notes."

"They'll wait long enough for you to spill."

"It's all so embarrassing, Rex."

"I thought we'd reached a point in our partnership where you could trust me to tell me even the most humiliating details about your life."

"Now you're trying to guilt me into talking."

"Is it working? Don't you want to get some of this story off your chest? You've been dealing with everything by yourself all this time. Or is there someone back in LA you've shared it with?"

Did he know how close he'd come to the truth? "Have you been investigating me on the side all this time?"

"No. Maybe I should have been, given your knee-jerk reaction to my questions."

She blew out a breath, her hackles relaxing. "You know most of the story. Thanks to the media, almost everyone knows. I was replaced on my own show, the ploy being to take the story back in time to a younger me. The producers' clever way of getting rid of me without coming right out and admitting they were firing me due to my age."

"Okay, that much I know. I didn't until after I met you. Then I went surfing on the Internet. I found quite a bit on you, although most of the stories carried the same details. No one appeared to have gotten the real scoop. Your publicist earned his money."

"Her money. That would be my manager, Jayne Yarmouth. Certainly not my agent, Deidre Mansfield. There was a brief period, after the news of my being out of a job broke, that I could've used the publicity to leverage new projects, but Deidre lost her nerve, hesitant to be associated with me. So I lost the momentum, and Deidre's lukewarm assistance worked against me."

Rex drew closer. "What does that mean? How did it work against you?"

She hadn't planned to share this part with him. At least not yet. They'd just sorta gotten there. She couldn't exactly beg off telling him anything, but what should she reveal? Rex wouldn't use it against her, despite how stupid she might come across. "Hollywood can be very fickle. One day you're the hottest property in town, and the next you can be avoided like the plague. Perceptions swing on a very unpredictable pendulum. Deidre's hesitation to go to bat for me sent off vibes I couldn't counteract. Bottom line, no one wanted me for their next project."

He folded his hands and leaned forward. "But surely you had friends in high places who could've helped you?"

"They did, but every time an interesting project came along, before we could seal the deal, it slipped away. Others in higher places saw to that, although I could never prove it."

"Why would someone do that?" he asked quietly.

"I don't know for sure, but my guess is that the producers who let me go didn't want the bad publicity, which they must've thought would happen if I emerged unscathed and in better shape than before. It sounds cruel and underhanded, which they'd only see as good business. My going on to something better might make them look like fools for letting me go."

"How long did this phase go on?" he asked.

"Months. Almost a full year from the day I learned I wouldn't be returning to Letitia. In the meantime, I had to keep up appearances. I went through most of the severance pay I got from them and then started on my own bank account. My late husband, Carson Grant, left me a sizable trust fund plus the properties we acquired during our marriage. I'd vowed not to touch any of them, but as I got increasingly desperate to make something happen, I modified my vow."

"How so?"

Was she ready to go into all that mess? She'd opened the door to it, but she could still back off now before she told him everything. On the other hand, telling someone else, someone she trusted, was already helping her feel like an anchor was being pried off her chest. "Are you sure you want to hear this? I won't come off very smart once you hear."

"I want to hear whatever you feel comfortable telling me," he said. "But if you want to stop now, I'll understand."

"Just when I was considering retiring from acting, a hero came into my life. At least that's how it seemed at the time. An actor I'd worked with early in my career who'd gone into directing and producing took me to lunch one day. He said he'd been holding onto a screenplay the last few years because it was perfect for me and I wasn't available. But now that I was, he thought this would be the perfect vehicle in which I could reveal the extent of my acting chops. I let myself get excited at the prospect before knowing much more about this property.

"He continued to build it up throughout lunch until I would've been ready to sign on immediately. And then he told me how close he was to having his financing lined up. 'Almost there,' so he said. Just needed a couple more million 'up front' and he could start production. He didn't come right out and ask me for it, but it was clear that's what he was after. I went home and called my banker. She advised me not to touch the trust fund. Instead, she suggested I consider unloading one or more of my properties, after she'd first lectured me on the wisdom of investing any of my own money in any acting project. I thanked her and called a real estate agent right after. Within a week, I'd sold the mountain cabin Hugo and I had bought early in our marriage when he needed to get away from Hollywood to write. I sold it for what I later to my horror learned for two million less than I could've gotten if I hadn't been in such a rush.

"But I got the financing my friend said was all he still needed. I transferred it to his account, expecting to hear my contribution was all that had been needed to get things rolling. Then I waited. And waited. At six weeks, I contacted him to find out the status, only to learn he'd switched to another project that had better legs. My investment was still intact, but I won't see any returns until this property is produced, released and makes back its seed money."

"I'm sorry," he said in all sincerity. "Is that the only way you can get it back?"

"I signed a release when I transferred my money, but I was so anxious to get the ball rolling, I didn't consult an attorney, who would've made sure I demanded and got some kind of risk mitigation clause in my contract."

They remained silent a bit as her words sunk in. They both realized the similarity of the situation she'd just described to the stories they'd been hearing the past two days from Elliot's victims. "I know what you're thinking, and I can't blame you. Even the fifty thousand Rita Haley handed over to Elliot is nothing compared to my foolishness."

He didn't say anything for a few beats, so her words hung in the air. "Is that why you agreed to help investigate?"

"Partially. After I learned I'd pretty much gifted my money to my so-called old friend, I became a bit of recluse for a while. Word of my folly remarkably didn't become widely known by either my circle of friends or the industry, mainly because it was still considered to be 'in play,' even though the new project was nowhere near underway. Somehow, Kitty got wind of my hermitage—although not my stupidity with the investment or my being on some kind of blacklist in the industry. She tried to convince me to come home for a while. I didn't take her up on her offer immediately because I didn't want to appear too needy to my own sister.

"I filed away my fiasco somewhere deep inside me to avoid comparing my situation to that of Scottie, Kaitlin, Rita, Arabella and Gordon Peters's niece, but I've only been fooling myself. It keeps rearing its ugly head. I understand their humiliation and desire to stay silent, but no part of me would've considered killing my friend. That's why I've had trouble believing they could do the same."

Finished with her story, she hung her head, not sure she wanted to know his reaction.

He didn't speak or move for some time.

His silence scared her. Had she lost his trust? At the very least, his respect?

At length, he did speak. "I don't know what to say, Marla. It's hard for me to picture you making a mistake of that magnitude, so you must've been going through the devil of a time since being released from your show. I'm sorry."

"Thank you. I appreciate your sincerity. That's a rare quality in my business. Working with you on this case has helped me put the LA investment blunder behind me. At least forget it momentarily."

"Thanks for sharing. If something connected to that project comes up where the input of a former police officer could help, let me know."

Tears had begun to form in her eyes, but she managed to stave them off. His words were balm to a still open wound.

She took a deep breath.

Time to move on. Break the mood. "Okay, let's take another look at those notes."

twenty-four

. . .

The police notes describing the crime scene were sparse. As they'd said all along, whoever killed Drake Elliot, whether it was planned or spontaneous, had done so leaving very little evidence behind. No footprints. No DNA; at least none had been found thus far. They hadn't even found the murder weapon. If it had been one of the larger rocks in the riprap surrounding the retention pond, it was nowhere to be found. Most likely it had been thrown into the water. The team that searched the water found several rocks on the bottom, but none had blood on them.

The first officer on the scene had canvassed every condo facing the front yard and pond and had found no one who had seen or heard anything from midnight to six in the morning the night Elliot was killed. That included Kitty, who'd promptly denied having any knowledge of what went down on the front lawn. That entry even included a note that said Kitty's sister, Marla Dane, was visiting at the time but was asleep throughout that period in a back bedroom.

"Did they check with you, Rex?" she asked, having read that part.

"No, but I'm on the back side of the building."

"But they just assumed I hadn't seen anything because of the location of my bedroom. For all they or Kitty knew, I might not have been able to sleep that night and had been out on the balcony drinking hot chocolate. Maybe while I was there, I saw something or someone."

"But you didn't. What's your point?"

"Suppose there actually was someone on the front side of the building who was out on their balcony and did see something. The officer on the scene only appears to have talked to whoever came to the door and depended on what they responded about anyone else in the condo. We talked about building management sending an email blast to all residents as a follow-up to the initial canvas. Maybe Goodhue should do it in a more official capacity," she said.

"Let's see what Goodhue and company can learn about Walker first," he replied. "Then we still have somewhere to go with the investigation if they learn nothing about her."

Marla returned to the notes. The police had immediately checked out his phone calls, emails, texts and credit charges. Early the morning his body was discovered, they were already contacting the four main restaurants he frequented. Three hadn't been much help. Although they remembered Elliot because he was a good tipper, they could only describe his dinner companions as females in their thirties to sixties. The fourth restaurant recalled the blow-up he'd had with his date that sent him walking and her paying for the meal. After a check of their records, they identified her as Scottie Richards. And the rest Marla and Rex knew from Scottie.

The police collected more names from his emails and texts, including Kaitlyn, Rita, Arabella Tansy, Noelle Donnelly and Donna Walker. "At least we've managed to talk to everyone he attempted to scam here in the building," Rex said. "And he doesn't appear to have been communicating with anyone else at the moment," Rex said.

"Guess he preferred to focus on one sphere of operations at a time," she replied.

"Anything else in the police notes jump out at you?" he asked.

"Just the lack of information. I can see why Goodhue decided to bring us on board," she replied.

He nodded. "Good observation. Could be because there was no other information to find or whatever there is is buried deeper than we've gone so far. Or it could be that Goodhue was right to acknowledge his staff could only go so far." He rubbed his chin, like that would help him discern more in the notes. "You know what I propose we do now?" he asked. "We let all the factoids and half-factoids floating around in our brains coagulate. I suggest a nap for both of us."

She wasn't expecting to hear that from big, strong, never-tired Rex Alcorn. "Uh ..."

"Not together. You'll know when and if I ever propose such a plan. Go back to your room at Kitty's and get some sleep. An hour or more. I'll call you if I hear from Goodhue."

How had he read her mood before she herself even realized she was exhausted? The last three days had been intense. She'd been "on" most of that time. Almost like when she'd been deep in her role of Letitia. Back then, she knew when a short nap in her trailer or even breaking for the day was in order. She'd forgotten how to take care of herself. His jibe about their taking a nap "together" if and when he decided didn't even ruffle her feathers. She was that tired. But she didn't totally forget the comment.

"Solved the case yet?" Kitty asked when Marla returned to her condo.

Ever since they were kids, Kitty had a way of downplaying

Marla's accomplishments. Long ago, Marla had dismissed her sister's lack of enthusiasm at such times as a little sister's way of coping with her big sister's successes. Her question now was probably part of the same type of behavior, although it could simply be sisterly curiosity. "We're getting closer. I'm home on a short break to rest my gray cells."

"You mean take a midday nap?"

"Okay, fine, a midday nap. I'll set the alarm on my phone for an hour."

"I'm going out for my painting class. You should be up long before I'm back."

The police notes came to mind. "Kitty? That morning after Drake Elliot's body had been discovered, did the police stop by here asking if we'd seen anything in the front yard the night before?"

"As a matter of fact, yes. You were still sleeping at the time."

"Did you answer for both of us?"

"Since the time frame they asked about was midnight to six in the morning, yes. I figured you'd been in bed all that time. You were, weren't you?"

"Yes, I was. I didn't know they stopped by, that's all. You didn't mention it."

"Sorry. Was it important?"

It was only connected to the very case she'd been working on, that's all. But no point mentioning that to Kitty. She'd only get defensive.

She woke feeling refreshed and ready to get back on the case. No messages from Rex yet. Well, it was Saturday, and crime-solving might go slower on the weekend, but she was hopeful something would break soon.

Might as well eat while she waited. Too bad Kitty's freezer didn't hold the same goodies as Rex's. In the end, she wound up making an omelet with shredded cheddar cheese and bacon. She couldn't believe how good it tasted. The fancy champagne breakfasts her personal chef prepared for her in LA didn't hold a candle to this simple fare. Maybe there were some benefits to this new life that had been foisted upon her.

An hour of sleep had gotten her going again. Food in her stomach brightened her mood.

As she ate the last bite of omelet, she received the text she'd been hoping for from Rex.

"What's up?" she asked when he opened his door to her.

"We've got some info on Walker. Seems the lady served time a while back for writing bad checks, so her fingerprints were in IAFIS, although not as Donna Walker. Her real name is Tammy Wyler."

"No wonder she didn't want to tell us much. Is there a warrant out for her arrest?"

"No, although Illinois has been watching her. Remember that clipping we found hidden in Elliot's condo? Turns out it was about the death of a resident in an Illinois medium security prison, Hal Cummings. He'd been suffering with COPD for a couple years, so it was a natural death. Four years ago, he'd been part of a huge investment scam involving thousands. It was thought he had at least one, maybe two partners who escaped detection, a man and a woman. But the authorities lost the trail on those two. The man, who at the time went by the name of Doug Evans, was in his late thirties. The woman was none other than Tammy Wyler."

Marla dropped into a seat. "That almost connects all the dots."

"If we can assume Elliot was Evans. So far, we have nothing tying him to the Illinois crimes. Although he has a record, it wasn't as Evans. He was only arrested. Never convicted. But his name came up more than once in the investigation that took down Cummings."

As she absorbed this news, two questions came to mind. "Where does Tammy Wyler fit into all this? If she's our killer, what was her motivation?"

"Tammy Wyler never showed up at Cummings's trial, but a woman that sort of fits her description did. The hair color was different, black, but the age was about right. Early thirties. Though Cummings received few visitors while in prison, he did get a lot of mail from a variety of men and women, but nothing was sent by a Tammy Wyler or a Doug Evans. It was thought, however, that Cummings and the woman involved in his crimes were a couple. The Illinois police speculate that she kept a low profile."

Marla attempted to see a connection with Elliot. "If this Wyler woman was in a relationship with the guy in prison, why come here?"

"My guess is that Elliot or whoever he was managed to get away with most or some of the money," Rex said. "And Tammy Wyler wanted it."

"Then why kill him?" she asked. "Unless she'd already gotten what she wanted from him?"

"By torturing him? There were no signs of such on his body, just that huge contusion on his head. I suppose she could've seduced it from him."

Marla couldn't help but laugh. "Wouldn't that have been ironic? If she did, how did she escape his knowing who she was?"

"He might not have ever met her," Rex said. "It's not like these crooks have meetings."

"Maybe she was trying to team up with him."

"Possibly, but partners don't usually begin their association with one offing the other," he replied.

She sat back and drummed her fingers on the kitchen table. The motion didn't help her figure out what had turned Walker into a killer, but it felt good to be doing something. "Even if we put all the pieces together, how would we ever get her to confess?"

"Good question. We need more hard evidence. Maybe that email blast from Goodhue will produce an eyewitness."

"That's a big maybe."

He sat back and folded his hands behind his head. "Yes, it is. But that's not saying we won't think of something else. Goodhue is having the Illinois people forward her file to us. Perhaps there's something in there."

"I don't think we have time to wait. Like you speculated before, now that we've talked to her, she's bound to take off. She's not the kind to travel with much baggage. She'll throw a few things together and disappear. Remember her interest in that back door?"

He pulled his hands back to his thighs. "What do you suggest we do?"

"My inclination is to show up at her door. Demand to talk to her again. But I'm not putting it forth yet. She'll just do what she did the first time, deny everything and keep her mouth shut. Or maybe not even answer the door."

"We have two choices: not confront her until we've got more on her and risk her taking off or confront her with nothing."

She considered their options, willing herself to come up with a third. But nothing occurred to her.

"Okay, something Goodhue said when I talked to him earlier might serve as a third choice," he said. "I didn't want to bring it up until absolutely necessary. Guess we've arrived at that point."

"What did Goodhue say?"

"He offered another set of ears if we wanted to run anything by him. He's never forgotten his desire to be a detective, same as me. He's sublimated his desires all these years by becoming a big boy, albeit in a small pond. Maybe we've overlooked something that he can spot."

She didn't take time to think it through. "Call him before we change our minds."

twenty-five

• • •

"I'm glad you called," Goodhue said after Rex explained why they'd chosen to consult him as they faced two seemingly unworkable options. "I was pretty sure we'd found our killer when I called you with the results of our checks, but like you, I didn't see a clear path to getting a confession from her."

"The question is, do we have enough to arrest her and prevent her from taking off?" Rex asked.

"Good question, Alcorn. We need our attorney's input."

"How soon can you get a decision?"

"It's Saturday. Let me see what I can do."

Rex shot Marla a look that said Goodhue's response wasn't positive.

"I know you don't want to hear this," Goodhue said, "but don't do anything involving Ms. Wyler until I get the word from our attorney, or we risk not being able to convict her."

Rex blew out a defeated breath. "Yeah, I was afraid you'd tell us something like that."

The line went silent. Then Goodhue spoke. "But, hey, if you're sure she's about to split, use your own judgment about attempting to stop her. But if you do, all I ask is that you let me know before you approach her. I want to have someone nearby to make the formal arrest if we get that lucky."

"How about that email blast we discussed earlier?" Rex asked. "At the time, we decided to hold off until we had more to go on."

"I'll get in touch with your building manager. With it being the weekend, I'm not sure she'll be accessible."

That shouldn't be a problem," Marla added. "When we spoke to her assistant this morning, she offered to help with whatever else we needed and specifically said she'd be available by phone and computer all weekend."

"Good. I'll take care of that immediately," Goodhue said. "I'll have all responses directed to me so you two can continue to keep a low profile amongst your neighbors."

"Well? Did we gain anything from that call?" Rex asked once they'd signed off.

"Just sharing our concerns with one other person who knows about this case relieved some of the strain I've been feeling," Marla replied. "But beyond that, we've got a direction to aim for. More than we had a few minutes ago, anyhow."

He cocked his head. "How's that? What did you hear that I didn't?"

"We've got his blessing to approach her if we think it's necessary. And if we think the time is ripe, we can use that email blast as our entrée."

"You really think someone will come forward and say they saw her out there crushing Elliot's skull?" he asked.

"Too bad the footage from the security cameras netted nothing," she said, thinking back through what she'd read in the case notes. "Funny, you'd think they'd have shown something, even if just a blur of two bodies moving through the area."

"CCTV footage doesn't lie, Marla."

She couldn't dispute that. But … wait! She pulled up the notes again. "It would appear the only video reviewed was for the cameras in the front lawn."

"Where the murder supposedly occurred."

"But there are other security cameras in the building. At the entrances and exits, the garage entrances and exits, the pool and game room areas. Since they aren't mentioned in the notes, does that mean they weren't checked?"

Rex regarded her with a strange look. "They should've been, but you're right. I don't recall reading anything about them."

"Time to visit the building manager," they both said at the same time.

Sanstrom was still out treating her migraine, but Iris Cadell was in the office. "The other security camera footage?" she replied when Rex asked her about them. "I don't think the police officer asked about them. If anyone checked them, it was Gretchen, because I didn't."

"We want to view them. Now," Marla told her, anticipating having to get Goodhue to intervene again.

But Iris Cadell surprised them. "I'm so sorry," she said, slamming her hand over her heart. "It should have occurred to us, but the young woman officer seemed to be in a hurry. I don't think she knew what she was doing. Someone, perhaps the chief, told her to check the security camera footage and she thought she was doing as ordered." She gestured for them to come into the inner office of the management suite.

Was it possible there was still evidence here to find? Marla couldn't believe such a major detail had been overlooked, but then, this must be one of those reasons why Goodhue wanted Rex and her on the job.

Within minutes, Rex and Marla were staring over Iris's shoulder at her computer screen. She started the footage at midnight. The lighting was poor and the background was mostly dark on the tapes from the entrance cameras. Only one person, a male dressed in dark work clothes who could have been any age from eighteen to sixty exited the building on the north end; a middle-aged couple left on the west end, but not before they both turned once they were outside and waved at someone inside the building.

From one to two, four people entered the south end of the building. Two guys in hoodies came in together with a small white dog following behind them on a leash. Not long after, a heavy-set guy in a dark uniform came in from the parking lot. Iris froze that frame so they could read the logo on the uniform. It was for a local delivery service. But he didn't appear to be dropping off anything. The fourth person, a woman who looked to be in her thirties, dashed into the building after being dropped off by a car. Only one person came in on the north end around one thirty, a woman in light scrubs, most likely a nurse, who was also dropped off by someone else who drove off immediately.

No auto traffic left either garage entrance after one, and only two vehicles returned, one around two at the west garage door.

"Is that all you've got?" a dejected Rex asked when Iris stopped the video at two o'clock.

"For the times you asked to see, yes," Iris answered.

Marla was just as disappointed as Rex. She'd been so sure they'd see something that would incriminate Tammy. "Maybe the medical examiner's estimated time of death was off just a bit. Run the garage entrance footage a little further."

"Okay. I'll start with the west garage door, since there were two vehicles that entered right around two."

"Slow it down, too," Rex said.

Iris did as asked. The seconds depicted on the tape dragged by.

Though she knew this was the best way to observe, the

snail's pace at which the tape now advanced was making Marla crazy.

Then, just as it seemed nothing would materialize, a male figure emerged from the building followed seconds later by a female figure.

"Go back to just before we see the first person," Rex said.

Iris was already on it.

It wasn't easy to make out much about the male because there was no light from behind him and only the light of the outside perimeter in the background that outlined his body.

Iris froze the screen. The man appeared to be wearing a dark dress jacket and dark pants, like he'd been out for the evening. They saw mainly the back of his head, short, dark hair. Only when he turned to the left was the side of his face visible.

"Is that him?" Marla asked the other two, having never met the victim, her heart beating wildly.

"Yeah," Rex breathed out. "That's our boy!"

"He appears to be limping," Iris said excitedly.

"Replay that part again," Marla said. How many times had she been asked to sit in on editing sessions when the director felt the day's filming hadn't met his standards and he needed a second pair of eyes to suggest what wasn't working. This was old hat.

She narrowed her eyes to get a better view. "Not limping so much as stumbling."

"We knew he'd been drugged," Rex responded. "Apparently it had already taken effect at this point. Let's check out that second figure."

Iris did as directed, this time freezing the frame before asked.

From the outline of the garment, it was clear it was a woman. With shoulder-length dark hair.

As she turned, her right arm was extended, pointing something. A gun.

"Donna Walker," all three of them shouted.

"She's chasing him," Iris stated the obvious.

They had her.

Marla clapped her hands together. Rex nodded vigorously. Without realizing what she was about to do, she hugged him.

Neither was in a hurry to come out of the embrace until Iris ahemmed. "Do I get a hug, too?"

"You did great, Iris," Rex said, offering her a hug as well. Much briefer than the one he'd shared with Marla.

"Does that video prove she's the killer?" Iris asked.

Marla exchanged looks with Rex. "Maybe not in court, but it gives us and the police the ammunition we need to confront her," Rex said. "But this is just amongst us and the police. Got that?"

"Oh, yes. I've never been in on a takedown before."

"Stay here in your office until we give you the all-clear," Rex told her.

Marla called Goodhue. "We've got her, Chief." She explained what they'd viewed. "A copy is being sent to you now. You'll see her chasing Elliot out of the building while aiming a gun on him at 2:04 a.m."

They waited while the chief downloaded the tape and played it.

"It's enough to bring her in for questioning," he replied. "Would've been perfect if we had her actually doing the deed, but this is almost as good. My folks and I can be there in ten minutes."

Rex, who'd been listening on speaker, intervened. "We can't wait that long, Goodhue. I sense she's ready to split any minute.

Marla and I can confront her and keep her occupied until you folks get here."

Marla held her breath. Both men wanted the capture. She wanted it, too, even though they knew Tammy Wyler had a gun. It was just the two of them against one woman. They should be okay, right?

"Be careful," Goodhue said. "Especially you, Marla. Just keep her talking. Don't try to be heroes, okay?"

"We've got this, Chief," Rex replied, for once acknowledging the other man's title. "But get here as soon as you can."

Marla hung up and involuntarily touched the pendant hidden underneath her shirt. "Ready?"

"Ready. How 'bout you? I included you without asking," he said.

She allowed herself a long breath. "Let's do this, then."

twenty-six

. . .

*D*onna/Tammy actually answered the door of her condo when Rex knocked. Without discussing her part beforehand, Marla stayed to the side and let Rex handle their entry. She tried counting to a hundred in her head to keep from picturing all the possible dire outcomes of this visit if this woman really was their killer. She'd put on a brave face for Rex, agreeing to come with him to face Tammy, but as soon as they got to the woman's door she'd had second, third and fourth thoughts.

Rex spoke before Tammy. "We're back with a few more questions, Donna, since earlier you took off without our being finished."

"I told you all I know."

"We've learned a few things about you we'd like to check," Rex said, sticking enough of his shoe in the door to keep her from slamming it shut.

"It's not a good time," Tammy replied.

"We won't take long," Rex said.

When his over-six-foot frame did not budge from the entry,

she relented, but not before releasing a heavy sigh. "Five minutes. That's all I can spare,"

Though she barely stepped aside, Rex pushed his way in. Marla followed in his wake, barely able to move her feet.

The living room was cluttered with her paraphernalia, which included a small hairdryer, various cans and bottles of hair product and a blond wig. Two small suitcases, a bag that appeared to be filled with groceries, a couple cardboard boxes and sealing tape and scissors were stacked on the coffee table.

"Going somewhere?" Marla asked.

"That's my business," Tammy replied.

"Our questions aren't scaring you off, are they?" Rex asked, edging even farther into the room.

Tammy stood her ground next to one of the suitcases. "Scaring me? No. I've told you several times I didn't know the man and know nothing about his murder. It's just time to be moving on."

"Then let's go over these questions before you go," Rex said evenly. "What is your real name, Donna?"

She blinked. "Donna Walker is my real name."

Rex nodded at Marla, indicating she should handle the next part. "That's not the information we have. Your real name is Tammy Wyler, although there may have been other aliases in between," she said. She used one of her Letitia voices, discovering the more she spoke, the less this probable killer intimidated her.

"Where, where did you get that?" Tammy replied.

Marla continued. "But your name's not the only false information you've been using. You don't work for Wentworth Enterprise and the former address you gave the rental agent for this condo is bogus."

One more blink. "So I made up a few details. There's no crime in that as long as I've paid my rent on time."

"No," Rex agreed, "but why the subterfuge?"

"I'm running away from an abusive relationship. I didn't want that jerk to find me."

She apparently had been prepared for this contingency. Time to get serious.

Rex took his turn next. "As Tammy Wyler, you did time in prison in Illinois," he said. "It seems you've developed quite a knack for bunco. Swindling investors into buying worthless property. Imagine that? From what we've learned about Drake Elliot, also known as Doug Evans, that occupation seems to have been what he excelled at. So why did you show up in town? Was he the so-called abuser or was it to join the team?"

"Or maybe you threatened to blackmail him if he didn't let you in on his game?" Marla added.

"I have no idea what you're talking about," Tammy replied,

"We have to credit you for tenacity, Tammy, but even you should know when it's time to bail," Rex said. "Thanks to the security cameras planted around the complex, we've got video of you chasing Doug Evans out of the parking garage at gunpoint on the very night and approximate time he was murdered."

Wyler didn't reply at first. Questioning whether Rex was blowing smoke?

"I've got a copy of that video on my phone if you don't believe me," Rex said, reaching in his pocket for his phone.

"I suppose it shows me out there on the lawn with him? Maybe you even have me raising my hand when he fell over and clobbering him with a rock I picked up from the riprap around the pond?"

Marla held her breath while Rex stared straight at Tammy. "Are you admitting that was you?" he asked slowly and deliberately.

She snorted. "If there was proof showing me doing any of

what I just described, the police would've arrested me immediately. But I'm still here."

Damn! Marla was sure they had her, but Tammy Wyler had been at this game long enough to know not to admit to anything where there wasn't absolute proof. Proof they didn't have and had been hoping to scare out of her. Maybe they just had to hold firm a little longer. "Funny you should say that. The police have never released what they suspect was the murder weapon, and yet, you didn't hesitate a second when you said you hit him with a rock."

"How do you know what the police have?" Tammy asked suspiciously.

Marla turned to Rex. This was his call. "Ms. Dane and I are working with the police at their request. How else do you think we've learned about your background as well as Elliot's or Evans, as I guess was his real name."

They waited for Tammy's response. Her expression had gone harder than the very stone she probably used to kill Elliot. She flinched. It only lasted a brief second, but they were ready for it. Anyone else might have missed it if they weren't attuned to the woman's every move. "What I said was just a lucky guess."

Marla didn't give up. "Mighty lucky, I'd say. You could've fooled me. I thought I heard a confession coming from you."

"Dream on, TV lady. You wanted a show. I gave it to you." Tammy headed back to open the door. "Sorry, folks. Show's over."

Rex beat her to the door and prevented her from opening it. "That was just the prologue. We figure you came here not just to find the money he supposedly stole from you and your boyfriend when your scam back in Illinois fell apart but also for revenge."

"Revenge?" she asked.

"When your multimillion-dollar scheme went south," Marla

added, "your boyfriend, Hal Cummings, got caught and went to prison for it. You managed to escape. So did Evans, and he had the money. Six months ago, Cummings died from a respiratory illness he'd had for years. Two months ago, you showed up in Minnesota, new haircut, new hair color. That wasn't just a coincidence."

"Where are you getting all this?" she asked incredulously. "You have no proof of any of it."

"That's where you're wrong," Marla said, now joining Rex near the door. "It's amazing what fingerprints can show these days. They write their own record of your past exploits and criminal charges. We've got you. Just try taking off. The police will be waiting."

Marla was writing her own script as she went, trying not to say too much but just enough to scare the woman.

She glanced at Rex for her next cue. In that flicker of a moment, Tammy ran to a nearby chest of drawers and removed a gun. "I don't need to listen to any more of your speculation. I'm getting out of here before you convince the police I killed him. You two, head back to the guest bath."

Foiled! They didn't have a backup plan for being held at gunpoint. All Marla knew was not to argue with a gun.

They appeared to have no recourse but to do as ordered, unless Rex overpowered her. And with his bad back, Marla dismissed that as an option as soon as it came to her.

"Step into that tub. Both of you," Tammy told them when they got to the bathroom.

Marla climbed in first, then Rex. Tammy nudged the roll of packing tape into Marla's stomach. "Start wrapping this stuff around him, mummy-style. Make sure you get it tight around his arms."

Marla had never imagined herself in such a dangerous and demeaning situation when she agreed to help Scottie. How had the tables turned on them so quickly? With a gun pointed at her she had little choice but to take the tape.

She started at Rex's shoulders and draped the tape around him. Her hands shook so much, it was difficult to complete each round, especially pulling it loose from the roll. The fact that she had to stand so close to the man didn't help her nerves, either.

"It's okay, Marla," he told her calmly.

Goodhue should be on his way. Just so he got there in time. It was not only mortifying to be standing in an empty bathtub almost on top of Rex but also awkward. If they didn't get out of here soon, it would be painful too.

"Gimme that roll of tape," Tammy demanded, after Marla brought the tape across Rex's ankles.

Marla handed it over. In order to mummify Marla, Tammy had to set the gun aside on the lavatory counter. If she'd been ready for it, Marla would have thrown herself at the woman in that instant while Tammy didn't have the gun. Maybe Letitia would have taken the chance, but Marla Dane was frozen in place.

Tammy didn't use as much tape on her as Marla had on Rex, but she managed to disable her arms and legs. Finally, she ripped off short pieces of the tape and placed it over each of their mouths.

"I won't say it's been fun, but seeing you out of commission in this bathtub comes close," Tammy said, pulling the shower curtain shut and then disappearing.

Immobilized and unable to speak, Marla fought not only to stay upright but to ignore how close she was standing to Rex. The scent of his after shave overpowered her nose. The rapidly increasing heart beat she felt beneath his shirt matched her own heart's progressively insane pounding heart.

She attempted to step back to give them both more room, but the slightest movement had her losing her balance and toppling over. She righted herself as best she could and continued to stay in the same position.

How long could they remain like this? She was already uncomfortable after a few minutes. Her legs were complaining and might give out at any time. The result could be disastrous. If she fell over, she'd probably take Rex down with her. Not good for his back, but especially not good for their partnership.

Tammy had shrewdly taped their mouths shut so they couldn't call out for help. Neither could they communicate with each other except with their eyes, and Rex was enough inches taller than her that she couldn't really see him. That left only their bodies to telegraph whatever was going through their minds, and the message she was receiving from Rex had her confused. Fear or excitement? *Don't go there, Marla.* Puzzling over that enigma wouldn't help at the moment. She had to focus on getting through this confinement.

A minute later, two gunshots rang out. They were close by, coming from somewhere within the condo.

Two meant it probably wasn't suicide. More likely, Tammy was attempting to shoot her way to freedom.

Marla glanced up at Rex, hoping he'd been better at interpreting what had happened, but all he did was close his eyes briefly.

A minute later, the door seemed to rumble as someone attempted to enter. Within seconds, it burst open and Goodhue stepped in. "Alcorn? Ms. Dane?"

He pulled aside the curtain. "Omigod! Are you two okay? Of course you're not," he said, answering his own question. "Let's remove that tape and get you out of there."

Before that happened, an officer stepped forward and took several photos. Probably necessary to build a case against Tammy but not exactly the kind of publicity stills Marla wanted.

Goodhue unwrapped Rex, and a female officer helped Marla.

Although the removal of the tape over her mouth hurt briefly, she was delighted to be rid of it. "We heard gunshots. What happened out there?" she asked, attempting to work her mouth again.

"Let's get out of this bathroom first," Goodhue said. "You two should probably sit down. Somebody get them some water."

Even though they had only been immobile a short time, walking out to the living room was an effort. Marla collapsed on the sofa and thankfully accepted a bottle of water from the female officer.

There was no sign of Tammy Wyler, although another officer was busy mopping up what appeared to be blood on the floor tiles.

"Okay, Goodhue. We're both fine. Did you get her?"

"Not without a fight," Goodhue replied. "She wouldn't let us in. Good thing we anticipated the gunfire. She shot right through the door. That's when Officer Linden here used her tactical hostage training to break through the door and shoot back at Wyler. I'd given orders not to use lethal force and just wound her. We want her alive so we can get as much information about Elliot/Evans as possible."

"So? It's over?" Marla asked.

Goodhue nodded gratefully. "The arrest phase, yes. All thanks to you two. You kept nibbling away at this case until you found enough evidence to get her to break. Now that we've got her in custody, she's starting to talk."

"Good! She's been a hard nut to crack," Rex said.

"Have to admit. I had second thoughts asking two civilians to pair up and help with this case, but you've both come through for me with better results than I had a right to expect."

Marla exchanged a look with Rex that sent her head

whirling. It hadn't just been a comrades-in-arms gaze. It had been something more. Something she thought she recognized, but it couldn't be, could it?

Rather than speculate about what had just occurred, she turned her attention to the chief. "I never thought I'd ever again find myself involved in a murder investigation when my stint on TV ended, let alone one involving a real homicide. I appreciate your confidence in me," Marla said sincerely. "But I couldn't have come close to learning who murdered Drake Elliot without Rex." Goodhue had challenged her to use what she'd learned subliminally in her role as Letitia and step beyond her reliance on someone else's words to solve this mystery.

"Marla held her own," Rex replied, that penetrating look still there.

"I'll let you two figure out who did the most," Goodhue said. "I need to get back to the jail. As far as I'm concerned, you made a pretty good pair of detectives. Who knows, I might just call upon you again. But let's hope it's not for another homicide."

epilogue

. . .

"You two actually captured the killer?" Kitty asked later that evening when all those they'd interviewed gathered in Kitty's condo to be brought up to speed.

"Everything came together today," Marla said.

"I was gone less than an hour to get groceries. Good thing, too, or we wouldn't have frozen pizza to celebrate with now."

"Which we appreciate," Rex told Kitty. "I brought what cold beer I still had in my fridge. Glad you thought to bring more, Gordon."

Gordon Peters opened his can. "No problem, Rex. I'm pleased to be included in this celebration. We're all waiting to hear how it went down."

"I thought I heard gunshots," Kaitlin said. "What was all that?"

"Gunshots?" Kitty said, surprised. "No one got hurt, I hope. Especially you two."

Rex gazed around the living room at those still standing. "Have a seat, everyone. Marla and I only want to go through this once. We've already spent enough time rehashing the story for the police."

"Thanks for bringing the champagne, Arabella," Marla said, passing around a tray filled with eight small plastic cups filled with the sparkly stuff. "Just what we needed to mark the end of this investigation and thank you all for helping us bring it to closure."

Rex began. "First off, her real name is Tammy Wyler. She changed it to Donna Walker along with her hair color and style and colored contacts when she came to Maple Knolls in search of Drake Elliott, who was really Doug Evans." He recounted how Tammy had been involved in a similar real estate investment scam along with Evans and another man back in Illinois. "Only that one involved even bigger stakes, in the millions."

Marla continued with the story. "By mid-afternoon we knew who she really was and were pretty sure she killed Drake Elliot. But we still didn't have enough to go on to turn her over to the police. When we confronted her earlier in the day, she'd denied even knowing Elliot. The email blast Chief Goodhue sent to building residents had so far netted no responses. We had to find some hard evidence. We feared she'd be picking up stakes at any time."

"That's when the woman who said she was finished playing detective got a brilliant idea," Rex said. "She reread the case notes and realized only the security camera video for the entrances and exits had been reviewed. Thanks to Iris here, we were able to review the footage for the garage entrances and exits."

A very excited Iris Cadell interrupted them. "And ta-da! There they both were on the footage from the west garage exit."

"Even though the lighting wasn't the greatest, we could tell one of the figures was the woman Rex and I talked to earlier in the day, Donna Walker, who we now know is Tammy Wyler,"

Marla said. "Rex and Iris identified the man she was chasing as Drake Elliot, who went by the name Doug Evans. I'd never seen him."

"We don't have actual footage of her killing him," Rex said, "but we do have her pointing a gun at him as she chased him from the building. Although we called the police immediately, Marla and I suspected she was about to bolt. We went to her condo before the police were able to get here."

"We confronted her with our evidence until she pulled a gun on us," Marla went on. "She never did admit to killing Elliot, but her actions were enough for the police to step in."

The group gasped at that news.

"Is that when we heard the gunshots?" Scottie asked.

"No. Luckily Marla and I weren't present for that part because she'd locked us in the guest bathroom to make her escape," Rex replied.

Marla shot a glance at him. "Tell them how she detained us."

Rex made a face. "Do I have to? Wasn't Goodhue finding us like that humiliating enough?"

Kitty leaned in. "Do tell. This sounds like the interesting part."

"The police have an official picture of us, Rex. Who knows how long before it's released to the general public?" She then described in painstaking detail how she and Rex had been temporarily mummified.

"Oh, how awful," Scottie said.

"How soon can we get a copy of that photo?" Gordon asked.

"How did you escape?" Rita now asked.

"Chief Goodhue and his force were in the hall waiting for some sign from us that we had her. When they didn't hear, they went to the door. Fortunately, per procedure, they stepped to the side until they breached the door. That's when Tammy used the gun she'd held on us to shoot through the door," Rex said.

"The second shot came from the police officer who took her down—wounded her," Marla said. "The rest you already know."

Kitty came over to Marla. "But you two are okay? She didn't hurt you?"

"Just our egos," Rex said.

"If she had a gun, why didn't she use it on Elliot instead of smashing in his head?" Kaitlin asked.

"We can only speculate about that. She held him at gunpoint to get him to reveal where he'd hidden her money," Marla said. "We know that much from what the security footage revealed. When he refused to tell her what she wanted to know, we're pretty sure she's the one who killed him. But the gun would've made too much noise."

"The same goes for the money some of you lost," Rex said. "The police as well as Marla and I searched Elliot's condo and came up empty as far as money was concerned. But we did find some coded information that is being studied by people who do that for a living. There's still hope."

"Will we get it back if they do find it?" Rita, the biggest loser in the group, asked.

"That's a question for the authorities," Rex replied. "We certainly hope so. If they do find it, you'll probably have to compete with the others he's scammed over the years and go through victim restitution."

No one seemed quite ready to leave after Marla and Rex finished debriefing the group. As they mingled in small groups, Scottie sought out Marla and drew her off to the side. "Thank you. I never dreamed you'd catch the real killer when I begged you to keep the police off my back, but you came through, Marla Dane. Not Letitia Carruthers. You, Marla Dane. You and Rex. I'll thank him later. For now, I just wanted you to know how much I appreciate what you did for me."

"Truthfully, I never dreamed we'd actually do it," Marla replied. "I'm just glad we did."

"I haven't forgotten our deal."

"What deal is that?" Marla asked.

"About contacting my friend in the business to find you a new project. I'll do that tomorrow."

Marla was used to promises that went nowhere. Sometimes even well-meant promises. That was just the nature of the business. Still, Scottie's heart was in the right place. No need to shut down her enthusiasm and gratitude. "Thanks. Do what you can. But in the meantime, I'm kinda getting to like this place." She took Scottie's hand. "Especially the people."

The group hung out for another hour asking variations of their initial questions. Kitty picked up on Marla's yawn and sent everyone home, including Rex.

"How about breakfast tomorrow?" Rex asked Marla on his way to the door.

"Uh, sure. Now that we've caught our killer, I thought our partnership had come to an end?"

"We need to debrief," he replied, not directly answering her question.

Once it was just the two of them, Kitty put her hands on Marla's upper arms. "I was serious about you needing time to catch your breath," she said. "Your brain and body have just survived some pretty nasty trauma."

"Okay, little sister. I'm off to bed." She hugged her back. "Thanks for taking care of me."

KITTY WAS RIGHT. Marla barely had her nightgown on before she fell asleep and crashed for the next seven hours. She woke around five in the morning, rose and used the facilities, drank a few sips of water and then fell asleep for four more hours.

Rex had already texted, suggesting they get coffee outside the building and not at the same place she'd met with Gordon Peters.

Before she met Rex, she asked Kitty to join her in the living room. "I never planned to get myself involved in a real-life murder case," she began. "But as it turned out, the experience was just what I needed to knock me out of the funk I was going through back in LA. Thank you."

Kitty sat back. "Thank me? What did I do? I certainly didn't stage an on-site murder."

"No, but when I agreed to help clear Scottie Richards's name, you supported me. Even when Rex Alcorn got involved. That means a lot."

"Wish I could take more credit, but I felt so out of my element, all I could do was be there for you and make sure you didn't get too carried away. Or get your heart broken by Rex."

That admission surprised Marla. "Did you really think that was possible?"

"Rex Alcorn has quite the reputation around here," Kitty said. "Even I found myself attracted to him at one time a few years back. Not that he did anything to encourage me. That's Rex. He comes across as the he-man no woman can resist. After several others had tried and failed to catch his attention, I decided I would be the one to succeed."

"And did you?" Marla had sensed something had gone on between her sister and her recent partner but hadn't been able to discern just what it had been.

"I thought I had, but Rex is just too nice to turn you down flat. Only when I started angling for dinner dates did he tell me he wasn't interested. My ego took a beating."

Marla started to reply that no, she and Rex found they

worked well together but nothing more had transpired. It hadn't, had it? No, of course not. Rex was just a good guy. After the jerks she'd worked with and dated in LA, it was a revelation to discover a man who didn't take advantage of her. "While we're on the subject of Good Guys, what's the story with you and Tom Casey?"

"Me and Tom?" Kitty returned a perplexed expression. "There is no story. He's just my neighbor. A good neighbor who's always there for me if I need anything. Where's that question coming from?"

How much was Kitty deflecting, or was she really unaware of her neighbor's concerns and feelings for her? "Tom seems to think there was more to your invitation for me to visit than you let on."

"I was concerned about you, Marla. Your manager, Jayne Yarmouth, told me you'd retreated from any kind of social contact. She suggested a change of scene would do you good."

"Jayne contacted you?" Jayne hadn't said anything about talking to Kitty.

"She's more than just your employee. She sees herself as a friend who really cares about you. You got a bum deal from those folks at your TV show, and she was at a loss how to help you past it, especially since the parts weren't coming your way."

"You know all about that?"

"Just enough to know you were suffering but would probably never let on to me how much. When I couldn't seem to get through to you, I asked Tom to call you and offer some story about my erratic behavior. That's why Rex has been acting so funny around me. He got wind of what I'd asked Tom to do and didn't approve."

"How did Rex find out?" Marla asked.

"He's Rex. He's all-knowing, or so he would have us believe."

"He hasn't said a thing about your deal with Tom Casey."

"Maybe, as much as he disliked our ruse, he started to understand what we had to do to get you out of LA," Kitty said.

"So you're fine? There's nothing going on with you that I need to be here for?" Marla asked.

"As fine as can be, I guess. There's always some drama going on in my life, but I like it that way. But now that you know, please don't use it as an excuse to return to that craziness back in LA. At least not right away. I like having you here."

Her sister's plea caught Marla off guard. She hadn't given a thought to returning to California until Kitty now mentioned it. "Not immediately, as long as you don't mind having me around? I could find a place of my own, I suppose. Temporarily, of course."

"And leave Rambling Meadows? You're just getting to know everyone."

"I don't know, Kitty. I don't want to cramp your style."

"Nonsense! Now that the Elliot murder has been solved, we can start doing things together."

"Uh ..."

Kitty must have sensed "doing things together" wasn't her greatest selling point. "Or you could follow through on that story you concocted for solving the murder and turn the experience into some kind of TV show."

A TV show? That had only been her cover story for talking to the various persons of interest. On the other hand ... Maybe? Perhaps even try her hand on a podcast, like Rex had suggested.

An hour later, Marla knocked on Rex's door for their debriefing, whatever that would be. They exchanged pleasantries on the way to a coffee shop of his choice. The subject of solving the murder didn't come up until they both had a mug before them plus a bear claw for him.

"Goodhue already called me this morning and updated me on what they've learned from Tammy Wyler after arresting her," Rex said by way of greeting. "We decided to let you sleep a little longer, but he said to call him later if you have other questions."

Though she was disappointed to have been left out of the call, she was also grateful for the extra sleep. The last few days had taken more of a toll on her body and psyche than she'd realized. Thank goodness Kitty had known.

"What did Chief Goodhue tell you?" she asked.

"We already knew or surmised most of it," he replied. "Though she was part of the insurance scam back in Illinois that put her lover, Hal Cummings, in prison, Elliot or Evans or whoever he was, never met her. That's how she was able to convince him she was a credible mark. When the police closed in on Cummings, Elliot disappeared with all the money. Cummings' s sister has been bankrolling Tammy's stay here for the sole purpose of getting their money back. That's why she hasn't been employed but could still afford to stay at Rambling Meadows."

That was all good background information, but it still didn't address the main question. "Did Goodhue and company get her to admit killing him?"

"Cummings's sister is paying for a sharp defense attorney who's advised Tammy not to admit to anything more than drugging Evans and holding him at gunpoint. That was only after Goodhue made them watch the footage of Evans stumbling from the garage with Tammy chasing him at gunpoint. Goodhue's brought in an assistant state attorney to continue with the interrogation, hoping the big guns will get her to confess."

"What's your take on the chances she'll crack?" she asked him.

He propped his jaw on his folded hands. "Hard to say. I was sure her pulling a gun on us and holding us captive was more than enough to prove she's guilty of the murder, but the state folks want to make sure they've covered all their bases."

"She's one tough cookie. Letitia would've gotten the confession by now, but that's just make-believe."

"How do you feel after what you went through yesterday?" he asked, moving onto their part in the investigation.

"Relieved. No, something a step up from relief. She could've used that gun on us, but she didn't. Instead, she bound us up in that shipping tape to prevent us from following her. Pretty elaborate way to slow us down."

"I don't think she planned on our catching up with her," he said. "At least not so soon or she would've grabbed a suitcase and left immediately. Instead, she took the time to box a few items. The tape was right there in front of her and probably a last-minute inspiration."

"My mind keeps wondering what would've happened if Goodhue and his people hadn't arrived when they did."

"Don't go there. We knew they were on their way. We also knew we couldn't wait any longer for them. Still, it took that extra bit of adrenaline, courage, to confront her. Which you used without hesitation."

"I can't believe I agreed to be part of this investigation without knowing more about police procedure. Letitia could've talked her way through the situation, but as I've said from the beginning, she's fictional. This was real life."

He put his mug back on the table and looked her directly in the eyes. "But you did agree. Why?"

She thought about her answer for quite some time. The immediate response that sprang to mind wouldn't cut it. Finally, she spoke. "I started to say that I wanted to help Scottie. And that was part of it. But if I'm honest, I agreed because I wanted to test myself against Letitia. I missed her, being her. I knew it was crazy to think I could do the same things a TV character did, but I lost so much of myself when I was fired, I wanted some of it back again."

Neither spoke for a bit. Her admission was still new to her, although somewhere in the back of her head, she'd probably known all along.

"Thanks for your candor," he told her at last. "I wasn't sure if you'd ever get there."

"You knew? The whole time?" She tried to process his statement but had to get past her amazement first.

He pulled one of those infrequent smiles. "Suspected. I'm good but not that good."

"The St. Paul police department will never know what a loss they suffered by not making you a detective."

His smile widened. "Thanks for saying that. It means a lot."

"Just telling you what I've observed."

"And whether you're ready to admit it or not, those powers of observation make you a pretty great detective yourself."

"For what it's worth," she replied, grateful for his kind words.

"Would you ever do it again?" he asked.

She laughed. "God, I hope not. At least not if someone in this condo complex was involved."

Now he laughed. "Yeah, perhaps that'd be a little too close to home. But Maple Knoll's a growing town. You never know."

"That's true. You never know."

afterword

Dear Reader,

Thank you for reading this book. If you liked it, won't you please take a minute to leave a review?

To keep up with Marla's new life in Minnesota, sign up for my newsletter at https://www.subscribepage.com/BBCozies.

This is my third cozy mystery series. I've also written seven books in the Nailed It Home Reno Mysteries series and nine books in the Mah Jongg Mystery series. You can learn more about them and also the eleven contemporary romances I've published on my website, www.barbarabarrettbooks.com.

Follow me on Facebook: https://bit.ly/2aXZvG9
Follow me on X: https://twitter.com/bbarrettbooks

sneak peek

Measure Twice, Murder Once

While you wait for Book 2 in the Unscripted Detective Mysteries, check out the first book in the Nailed It Home Reno Mysteries, *Measure Twice, Murder Once*. Like Marla Dane, Rowena Summerfield is a take-charge woman in her mid-years who finds herself pulled into the arena of homicide investigation when her plans were to do something else.

EVEN THOUGH THE AWNING HUNG at a precarious angle, I could still envision how this place must have looked at one time. Then it hit me. "The only reason for that metal canopy is to block anyone in the rooms up on the second floor from gazing down here."

Val studied the structure a bit longer. "That theory makes sense. But why?"

"Something was obviously happening in here that whoever occupied the above rooms wasn't supposed to see."

"Like what?" she asked. "Drug deals? Meetings with crooks?"

My imagination had been piqued. The old detective

mentality emerged. Those two scenarios were possible, but why here? With so many rooms in the house, why not somewhere inside? Unless someone wanted to be outside but unseen? The naked sunbathing theory came close to answering the question, except for the awning. But the idea of nudity hung in my mind.

Then it hit me. Good grief, it couldn't be. If I was right, no wonder the place had been such a bargain. How would Val's reemerging hold up when I shared my suspicion?

Val noticed. "Mom? What are you thinking?"

I tried to dismiss her. I didn't want her self-confidence to backtrack. "Never mind. It was a crazy thought."

But Val wasn't one to give up easily. "Try me. How crazy?"

I knew I couldn't hold out on her. It would be easier to share what I suspected and for her to laugh it off than have her keep bugging me. "I need to read that abstract to confirm my theory, but all those tiny rooms throughout the house, the sickening smell, that disgusting wallpaper and now this *private* area—I think this place may not have been a family home at all. I think it served another purpose."

"What?" By now she was almost screaming with curiosity.

"I, uh, think we've bought ourselves a brothel."

Learn more at
barbarabarrettbooks.com/nailed-it-home-reno-mysteries/

acknowledgments

This book would not have been possible without the input and suggestions of my editor, Chris Kridler, of Sky Diary Productions. Chris also produced the incredible cover, formatted the manuscript and enhanced the back cover blurb.

Thanks also to Sharleen Newton, Harriet Sawyer and Bernadine Marsis for their keen proofing eyes.

As always, thanks to my husband, Veryl, for his ongoing support.

BOOKS BY BARBARA BARRETT

COZY MYSTERIES

The Mah Jongg Mystery Series

Craks in a Marriage

Bamboozled

Connect the Dots

Beware the East Wind

Flower Power

Jokers Wild

The Charleston Challenge

The Dragon Lady Gets Her Due

Courtesy Call

also available in paperback

Nailed It Home Reno Mysteries

Measure Twice, Murder Once

Loose Screw

Death by Drywall

Homicide by Hammer

Nuts and Bolts

Snared by the Snake

Wrenched at the Reindeer Run

The Unscripted Detective Mysteries

Curtains for the Condo Casanova

A LITTLE ABOUT
BARBARA BARRETT

Barbara Barrett started reading mysteries when she was pregnant with her first child. When she'd devoured as many Agatha Christies as she could find, she branched out to English village cozies and Ellery Queen. Later, to avoid a midlife crisis, she began writing fiction at night when she wasn't at her day job in human resources for Iowa State Government.

After releasing eleven full-length romance novels and two novellas, she returned to the cozy mystery genre, using one of her retirement pastimes, the game of mah jongg, as her inspiration. Not only has it been a great social outlet, it has also helped keep her mind active when not writing. She has written nine books in her Mah Jongg Mystery cozy series that features four friends who met each other when playing mah jongg and now find themselves tracking down killers even though they've never received formal investigative training.

Though not an interior designer, that occupation has always fascinated Barbara. Her father was a carpenter and her husband has his own woodworking business. Exposure to their work got her interested in watching numerous home improvement shows on HGTV. Ro and Val, her characters in the seven books in the Nailed It Home Reno Mysteries series are an amalgam of several HGTV hosts. Barbara used that combination of personality traits for Ro and turned her into a female sleuth who also rehabs older houses.

Barbara is a member of Sisters in Crime, Sinc-Iowa and Florida Star Fiction Writers.

She is married to the man she met her senior year of college.

They have two grown children, eight grandchildren and two great grandchildren.

Now retired, she is a resident of Iowa and also spends time in Minnesota. She earned her B.A. degree in History from the University of Iowa and her Master's Degree in History from Drake University.

When not in front of her laptop creating her next story, she plays mah jongg, watches TV detective shows and enjoys lunches with friends. Most recently, she has begun to paint in acrylics and is working to evolve her skills.